NIKKI PRINCE

Evernight Publishing

www.evernightpublishing.com

ONCE UPON A DREAM: VOLUME ONE

ISBN: 978-1-77130-575-4

Cover Artist: Sour Cherry Designs

Editor: Marie Medina

NIKKI PRINCE

WAKING BEAUTY

DEDICATION

Waking Beauty would not be in existence without the following people. Shyla Colt who gave me the first initial shove. Elyzabeth M. VaLey for helping me with my Spanish and encouraging me. Doris O'Connor and Melanie Fletcher in encouraging me to go for it with the BDSM aspect.

Thank you girls! I love you all!

NIKKI PRINCE

WAKING BEAUTY

Once Upon a Dream

Nikki Prince

Copyright © 2013

Chapter One

Aurora shook her head and had to stop herself from rolling her eyes as she listened to the doctor basically tell her all the things she already knew. She was a workaholic. The lack of sleep mingled with those long hours she worked would make the strongest person collapse.

"Just tell me what I need to do so that I can get back to work."

"Plain and simply put, Ms. Devine, you need to get some sleep and some relaxation, and then you need to have one long orgasm."

"Dr. Fairee, you can't seriously mean what you just said." She looked at him and watched as he leaned forward to gaze at her from behind his desk.

"I mean every word of what I just said. You've told me your symptoms, and I'm telling you the cure. Lack of sleep, always working, and you haven't had an orgasm by a man's hand in … what was it? A hundred months, you said? Which equals eight years and four months too many, you said?"

She sighed. He was repeating word for word what she'd said, so she knew he'd been listening.

"Yes, that's what I told you, but…" The doctor held up his hand and looked at her over his glasses.

"No buts, Ms. Devine. You came to me for help, and I'm going to help you." She could have sworn she saw a twinkle in the old man's eyes. She shook her head to clear it; it felt so foggy.

"Now … you're going to take every bit of my advice, and we will have you cured in no time and screaming out some young man's name like no one's business."

If she could still blush that comment would have made her. She opened her mouth to speak; however, Dr. Fairee held his hand up as he looked at her with the wisest grey eyes she'd ever seen. There was something about him that tugged at her memory, but what it was she couldn't say. Her last doctor had suddenly moved away, and this doctor was the only one with openings so she'd acquired him.

"You're a beautiful woman, healthy otherwise in all areas except this. Trust me to know what you need. You pay me enough." A grin spread across his face and she couldn't help but smile herself.

She relented. "Then what do you suggest I do?" The doctor began looking through what appeared to be a business card holder.

"Ahh, here it is, just the thing you need and just what the doctor ordered." He held up a card that in the light seemed to shimmer with a golden hue. He held it out to her, and she took it from him.

The only thing on the card was a drawing of a spindle—nothing else—though it seemed to gleam oddly. "A spindle?"

"Right, it's for you to decide your fate."

"Okay, where's my doctor and what have you done with him?" Though he'd only been her doctor for the last few months, Doctor Godwin Fairee had never talked this strangely to her before. Why was he doing so now? Had the older man knocked his head on something?

"Humor me in my old age."

She sighed. "Okay, so what am I supposed to do with this?" She waved the golden card around in the air as she spoke.

"Look at the card, my dear. I'm sure you missed something."

She glanced down and sure enough written in the deepest red were these words, *Once Upon a Dream Fantasies: Where we bring out the O in orgasms.* She glanced up quickly and looked at him. She knew there was a frown on her face.

"Okay, you can't be serious. Did you have these cards made up just for me?"

"Now you can't be serious." He had a small grin on his lips. "Just for you? No, there are others who need such a push too. The worse cases I send there." He pointed to the card in her hand. "It's a set up where you can have your fondest wish given to you in order to help you with the issue at hand."

She closed her eyes. This seriously had to be a dream.

"I'm afraid closing your eyes won't help the situation. On the other hand, facing your need head on will."

She opened her eyes and stared at him, really regarded him. "So what happens, I just make a wish and poof all my problems will be gone?" She knew she sounded sarcastic.

"Nope, not saying that at all, you will have to work for what you want. Your wish for that elusive orgasm will be fulfilled in any way you wish. Your destiny is just that, your destiny." The doctor sat back in his chair with his hands under his chin.

This all sounded so crazy. Perhaps she was sleeping. She reached over and pinched her right arm and the sting of pain let her know that she was very much awake. What's the worst that could happen? *Well, you could find out that the doctor you've been paying money to is a crazy old flake. What if he isn't?*

"Okay, so I'm not asleep. How do I do this?"

"Flip the card over and call the number on the other side."

"I have to do this today?"

"What are you waiting for? Didn't you tell me you had some vacation coming?"

"Yes, yes, I did and I do." She nodded.

"Well then, I say you call as soon as you can. Though that is all up to you, I'm not trying to be part of the problem but part of the cure." He chuckled.

She got up out of her chair and strolled over to the large window in his office. The blinds were open and she stared out into the brightness of the day. To be able to just let go was an aphrodisiac in itself. He was her fondest erotic dream. Immediately her thoughts went to Felipe Santiago Castro.

She clenched her legs together trying to ease the ache that she immediately felt when she thought of him. He made her wet and needy and he wasn't even around. He hadn't been for a long while. His absence was something she'd always felt deeply. She'd left him and not under the best of circumstances either. As a control freak, she'd balked at the idea of having him control every aspect of her life and taking care of her. What had scared her most was the fact that she'd wanted him to. He'd argued that it didn't make her weak and in the end she'd run from him in the middle of the night.

Her leaving had signaled her troubles in more ways than one. The way he'd made her feel had scared her. The relationship she'd had with him took on a life of its own in every aspect. She'd lost herself in him, and she hadn't been ready for that. In the end she'd thrown herself into her work once he was out of her life.

His absence, though all her fault, had left a void. Aurora was brought from her thoughts as the card she held in her hand seemed to warm up. She glanced down quickly to stare at it. It still had that odd shimmer. She wanted to feel what she'd felt with him, even if only for a few nights.

"Stop stalling and call, Aurora," he urged.

"Okay, I'll call as soon as I get home."

She turned back to him. She'd made up her mind, she'd do it. Hell, if this turned out to be a joke he was the only one that would know about it and she could walk away. The expression on his face told her that he thought she was procrastinating. He held out a cell phone to her. *Wow, he was that serious he was going to let her use his personal cell? Well alright then.* She walked over to where he sat and reached over the desk and took his phone, offering up a thank you. He waved his hand towards the phone.

"Damn, okay, okay, I'll call now."

"Good."

Turning back to the window she flipped the card over and dialed the number at the back of it and waited while it rang.

"Once Upon a Dream, where all your fantasies become a reality, this is Shae, how can I help you?"

"Um yeah, I'm calling at the request of Doctor Godwin Fairee."

"Oh yes, Ms. Aurora Devine, we've been expecting your call."

"You have, have you?" She peered over at the physician and he shrugged.

"Yes ... we have." The woman on the other side of the phone said in a singsong voice. *Man, could the woman be any more cheerful?* She couldn't help the small chuckle.

"So where do I go from here?"

"We'd like you to come down to the club by 11:30 pm this Friday evening. You need to be there early, as there is paperwork that needs to be filled out and it will give you enough time for everything that starts at midnight. You won't need any changes of clothing, as it's not required that you wear any. If you are uncomfortable with that, there are robes that will be provided for you." *Midnight, Friday and no clothes? This Friday was only four days away and it was the day she was starting her vacation. How convenient.* She shivered at the naughty possibilities of being in a club that was clothing-optional.

"Midnight?" It was the only thing she could think of. There were so many questions and it being midnight was the least of her worries.

"Yes, Ms. Devine. Midnight, it's when wishes work best."

She glanced at the doctor who still sat calmly at his desk, his face still holding the same expression of before. He raised his eyebrow at her as if to say, 'well?'

"Alright, I'll be there at the time requested. Can you tell me exactly where this club is?" The woman rattled off the address and it was an area that Aurora knew. She then gave her some more instructions and politely asked if she had any questions. Aurora told her no, and the conversation ended with a cheerful goodbye from Shae and the dial tone of the phone. She thanked her then hung up the doctor's cell.

She walked back to the desk and held her hand out to the doctor and shook it.

"Thanks, Dr. Fairee, I'll see you in a few weeks?"

"I'll always be around if you need me, Ms. Devine." What a bold promise from a doctor who should have a lot of patients. If he wanted to be at her beck and call, she'd let him.

He shook her hand firmly then let it go. Grabbing her purse she turned and left the small office building to head home. If she was going to do this, she'd do it with a bottle of her favorite moscato for some courage.

NIKKI PRINCE

Chapter Two

Aurora sat in her car as she gawked at the large building that spread out for several blocks and wondered for the hundredth time why she'd agreed to do this. The building, though huge, just didn't seem like a place where dreams came true. Perhaps the good doctor was a flake. Although she'd never know if she chickened out, right?

She turned off the car, grabbed her keys and tossed them in her purse and got of the car, locking it before she changed her mind and went back home. The parking lot was filled with cars so that must mean something. When she arrived at the gate she was met by the largest man she'd ever seen standing at the door with his arms across his chest. He peered down at her.

"Name please." He held up a clipboard.

"Aurora Devine." God, he was intimidating to look at, tall, well built with a shaven head and a fiery colored goatee.

"There we go. I see your name and you're expected. Go in and turn to the left. You'll find reception there." It was all he said before he pressed the palm of his hand against the large wooden door, holding it open for her.

"Thank you." She slipped past him and stood in the entrance way for a moment letting her eyes adjust to the difference in lighting.

From her vantage point at the door as far as she could tell there looked to be two different dance floors, several bars throughout, chairs and tables lining the walls and floors and every square inch had people. People in various states of undress; some were completely naked and others in robes. A thrill shot through her as she thought of the possibilities. The second, third and fourth levels had stairs with a balcony and rooms. What the rooms were used for she couldn't tell. No, scratch that, she knew exactly what they were used for. It basically looked like a really large five-star hotel with all the amenities one could ever want.

She turned to the left and headed for the desk that she'd been instructed to go to, though she still didn't know why she was there in the first place. *Oh yes you do, you want to be able to feel again. Anything for someone, something.* She brushed those thoughts away and smiled at the woman behind the desk. The blonde smiled at her.

"Ah, you must be Aurora."

Aurora knew her mouth was hanging open. "How'd you know that?"

"Because everything here is done by invitation only, I'm pretty efficient at my job. I know everyone who's coming in to have a wish or two fulfilled."

Aurora swallowed hard. What did she get herself into?

"Okay, this is what happens now. I can see that you want to run out before acquiring what you came here for."

Aurora started to protest but the grin that came over the woman's face told her it would be useless.

"First things first, I'm Flora, the hostess here. So this is what I need from you. You need to leave your purse and cell with me. I will lock it up in a safe deposit box. Then you will fill out this questionnaire and waiver and the fun will begin."

Aurora glanced one more time down at her purse and then handed it over to Flora. Flora set it down on the desk then handed the clipboard to Aurora. Next to the desk was a chair so she just slid into it and settled down to look over the questionnaire and waiver. Before she thought too deeply she just filled everything out, not even trying to second guess what half of it meant. If she did, she wouldn't be able to go through with it. Done, she stood and handed the forms back to Flora.

Flora glanced over the paperwork then smiled. "Fantastic, you've picked one of our most popular packages."

"You mean there are others who have the same problem I do?"

"Not necessarily the same problem as you, it's just that the 'Fantasy Stimulus package' offers a lot."

"What exactly do I get with that?"

"Your fondest wish, my dear. Now what I need you to do is to follow Dante up to your suite." Flora was just as vague as the paper had been. Truth be told it had intrigued her that there hadn't been anything said about what she would get, other than it was the most sought after package and she wouldn't be disappointed.

"A suite? There are suites here?"

"Godwin Fairee made it possible for you to have our biggest and most comfortable room. He said we should spare no expense." Aurora chuckled and shook her head. He'd said that, had he? "So as I was saying. I need you to follow Dante. He will take you up there and leave you in the capable hands of your fantasy date." Flora nodded her head in the direction where Dante had mysteriously appeared. It was like everyone was a fucking ninja around there. She hadn't even seen him show up.

"That fast?" She wrung her hands together, getting a bit nervous.

"Isn't this what you wanted, Aurora? To have every fantasy fulfilled, and what was it? She glanced down at the clipboard. "Have your prince come and sweep you off your feet, giving you everything you could ever want sexually?"

It was true. She'd filled out the questionnaire stating she wanted to be taken over fully and completely and loved as she'd never loved before. She'd even gone so far as to describe her prince as looking like Felipe. She clenched her thighs together again. She needed to come, though not by her hands anymore. She wanted a man to give her satisfaction. Most specifically a certain man but that's what fantasy were for.

"Have you changed your mind, Ms. Devine?" Had she? No. If there was one thing she wasn't that would be a coward. She'd see this through.

"No, I'll go with Dante and comply with whatever is put before me."

"Sounds like a wonderful plan." Flora stood and held out her hand.

Aurora stood as well and shook Flora's hand and then turned and followed Dante. Tonight was going to be a night of many surprises she hoped and a night of finding herself right along with her pleasure. She couldn't let the fact that it would be sex with someone she didn't know bother her. It had been too long and on a scale from one to ten on the need factor she was a blazing eleven.

She wanted to forget. No, she needed to forget. If she could just get past the memories perhaps she'd be able to let go and have that one mind-shattering orgasm and then she could go back to normal life. Dante led her up the stairs to the balcony and she felt as if every eye in the place was on her. Hell, everyone was here for the same thing so she shook off the embarrassment. She squared her shoulders as Dante stopped in front of a door and moved to the side after he pushed the door open. Candles brightened the room, giving it a soft glow.

Walking farther into the room she paused to take in every little nuance that was the fantasy suite. The furniture in the room was all made of cherry wood and the bed was a large canopy bed in the middle of the room. The comforter and pillows were a mixture of gold and brown tones.

Everything in the room was lush and all they could possibly need was within that room as well. Aurora noted the shiny foil packets on the nightstand, the one long red stemmed rose in the vase, the large bottle of champagne chilling in the bucket along with the tall flutes. She turned when she heard the clearing of a throat. It was Dante.

"Your stimulus package will be here in a fifteen minutes. Your instructions are on the bed." With those words he closed the door behind him, leaving her in the candlelit room. The door closed behind Dante, and she made her way to the pristine note that was laid out on the bed. Picking up the paper she scanned it carefully, wanting to make sure that she followed everything to a tee.

Dear Aurora,

In order for me to provide you with everything your heart desires, these are the instructions you must follow.

1.
ou need to undress completely. Place your clothes in the closet.
2.
n top of the pillow is a red blindfold. Put it on.
3.
ake sure you're settled on the bed.
4.
o not touch yourself. That's my job. I'll know if you do, and there will be consequences.

I'm looking forward to our time together. I hope you are too.

Sincerely,

Prince Charming

She couldn't help having a silly smile on her face as the words from the letter washed over her. This place seriously wanted to keep everything in the realm of fantasy. It was even signed by Prince Charming.

Aurora glanced at her watch; she had about ten minutes to spare, enough time to get undressed and ready as she'd been instructed. She wasted no time. Quickly divesting herself of her clothing, she hung them up in the closet. Every bit of clothing was gone. She wouldn't leave anything to chance.

Her Charming had requested that she be completely nude and she'd make sure to do just that. She climbed up into the bed and placed herself right in the middle, pressing her legs together in anticipation. She was past due for this. Yes, she could get herself off, but she wanted the touch of a man. Someone who would take care of every need she had.

Her nipples were aching and before she knew it, she cupped her breasts in her hands and closed her eyes on a deep sigh. Her juices pooled between her thighs, and she squirmed to ease the ache. Tentatively she cupped herself between her legs and rocked into her fingers. Her juices coated her fingers. That eased the ache a bit. If only for a moment and then she remembered that she wasn't supposed to touch herself. She snatched her hands away and picked up the red blindfold and slipped it over her eyes. It was secure, so she couldn't see anything.

There was silence, except the sound of the beating of her heart in eagerness of her Prince coming. She didn't have long to wait. The creak of the door opening informed her that she wasn't alone.

Chapter Three

The quiet continued on for a few moments longer before finally she couldn't stand it any longer.

"Are you there?"

"Yes, Beauty, I'm here." The voice was deep and the accent Spanish. They'd given her what she wanted. It wasn't Felipe, nonetheless he'd do. She could pretend it was him. Only Felipe could make her come. The fantasy, if kept alive in her mind and in her heart, would make everything okay. She had to believe that. She couldn't continue the way she was going. Hopefully just dreaming of Felipe as she was being touched would be enough.

She let herself live in the fantasy. This wasn't a random stranger: it was her Felipe and he'd come back for her.

"I see you followed all of my instructions to the letter with exception of one." His voice was stern and she squirmed.

"I...I..."

She heard the tsk-tsk that he gave. "Don't bother to explain. I told you there would be consequences, didn't I?"

"Yes, but?" How on earth did he know she'd touched herself?

"No buts, Beauty. When I give my word I mean every bit of it. So you will be punished. There is no other way around it. I give what I promise."

His words exhilarated her and at the same time scared her. This was what she wanted and he was going to give her exactly that. He reminded her of Felipe in so many ways. "Now ... do you understand, beauty?"

"Yes, I understand..." She didn't know what to call him. From what she could hear he was moving about the room and he hadn't tried to touch her yet. It was making her antsy.

"You should know what to call me. What did you put down on your paperwork?"

"I put Amo and señor." Those two words were what she'd placed on the form. Amo and señor were what she used to call Felipe. Amo meant master and of course señor meant sir. She did say she wanted this to be as real as possible. This place didn't half step at all. They followed everything that the client wanted.

"Then that is what you call me when you address me, Aurora. Is that understood?"

"Yes, señor, I understand."

"Perfecto, my beauty."

Damn, she really could believe it was Felipe. The accent was to die for. She let out a startled gasp as she was picked up by strong hands and held against an even stronger feeling body. In the next moment she was laid across his lap on her stomach. His fingers swept over her lower back where she had her tramp stamp.

"What a beautiful tattoo, Aurora."

"I got it on a whim, señor." It was vines on either side with thorns and a rose that dipped into the middle near her ass.

"Briar Rose," he whispered softly. His words were so light that she almost thought he was talking to himself. His fingers traced lightly over the tattoo and then there was a stinging slap to her ass.

"What are you doing?" She couldn't help the startled gasp that escaped her as the sting from his palm resonated through her whole body. Her words were given in her shock.

"I think you know what's happening." His palm rested on her bare ass and she squirmed.

"Stay still." The command was given and she immediately obeyed. His large hands stroked slowly over her ass.

"What instruction did you disobey, Aurora?" All the while he rubbed his hand over her bare bottom as he spoke. It was soothing as much as it was delicious.

"To not touch myself."

"That's right, my beauty." She squealed from the first smack on her ass by his palm.

"While you're here, this is my ass, my pussy and my breasts." With each word he slapped his hand against her backside, making her moan. Her butt was stinging from the spanking. Granted, it was in a pleasurable way. This paddling didn't repulse her. In fact, she wanted more.

"Do you understand, beauty?"

He gave her another rapid succession of slaps against her bottom. She found herself rocking her body into his lap.

"Yes, yes, señor. I understand fully." Her ass was burning as she was being spanked as if she were a petulant child, and she loved it. Each slap set off an electric current of sensations that went straight to her clit.

"Do you? Tell me what's mine, repeat it."

"This is your ass, your pussy and your breasts, Amo." He rubbed his hand over her posterior as if to soothe the burning sensation he'd caused.

"Si, all of you. Your body is mine, don't forget that." He gave her one last smack to her ass then settled her back on the bed. She wasn't sure if he left her in the middle of the bed or if he sat her near the edge. She stayed perfectly still. Since she couldn't see she tried to hear what he was doing.

The bed moved a bit and then she heard some drawers opening and closing, those sounds informing her that he'd left the bed. She stayed on her knees with her hands resting on her legs. She felt her juices running down her thighs. She was extremely wet, which was a good sign.

"You're in the middle of the bed, beauty. Lay back and relax on your back. We are going to play a little game."

"A game, Amo?" Not wanting to disappoint him she settled back on the bed

"Si, a game."

He didn't elaborate, and she didn't want to delve further into it. She needed to go with the flow. This wasn't work where she had to be in charge. That had been her problem over eight years ago. Not allowing Felipe to take control of her life in all aspects had ruined their connection. She was going to let go of the control that she always held on to tightly. Felipe had been right. She craved his control. It was just too bad that she realized it too late.

Once more she felt the bed depress and then he was speaking to her.

"Rise up. I'm going to put a pillow up under your hips." She did as he requested, no questions asked. When the pillow had been placed under her, she relaxed. His quietness was unnerving. Aurora was sure there was a reason for everything he was doing.

"Your pussy is beautiful, Aurora."

She groaned as he teased his hand over the top of her bare mound. It was a throwback from her time with Felipe. He'd loved her shaved and had told her that was how he expected her to be. He wanted her easily accessible to him, so that he could readily tease her whenever he wanted. She bucked against his fingers as he stroked her clit.

"So responsive, it's truly a mystery to me why you're here."

"You read my paperwork, Amo. You know why I'm here."

"Yes, you're right. I want to hear it from your lovely lips."

God, he was torturing her. She whimpered, trying to arch as close to his teasing finger as she could.

"I'm here—" She cried out as he slid his finger along her slit, teasing her entrance yet not pushing within her as she wanted.

"You're here because?" The brush of fabric against her inner thigh was enough to let her assume he was already naked and wearing a robe. Excellent. Perhaps he would just fuck her and she could get that long awaited orgasm or two.

"Oh fuck!" She sobbed.

"Yes, we're definitely going to fuck. Though not right now and it will be even longer if you don't tell me what I've asked of you."

"No, please, señor. I'm here because I need to relinquish control and I need to come." She knew she was begging him. She wanted this desperately. Even with such a short time with him, not seeing his face, with the illusion she wanted him badly.

"You look ready to come right now. In fact if I slid my fingers inside you and finger fucked you, I'm sure you'd come really well."

"Then please, Amo, do it." She urged.

"Ahh, Aurora, my dear. If I gave in to you that easily, what fun would this be and what lesson would be learned?"

"Lesson?"

"Mhmm, there is always a lesson to be learned, my dear." She gasped at the flick of his tongue against her clit.

"You taste wonderful. Now relax yourself. And let the game begin."

Oh my god, he didn't just tell me to relax? He has me wound up tighter than a spring. She took in a deep breath, trying to do as she was told to do.

"I can't relax with you doing that to me."

There was another flick of his tongue against her clit and then he wrapped his lips around it and suckled hard. She almost shot off the bed in her pleasure. Her hands gripped the cover on the bed tightly as she rocked into his mouth.

Just as it was getting good he removed his mouth and tongue from her, leaving her wanting. She let out a sob in frustrated need.

"Spread your legs wide."

Wanting to do whatever she needed to do to get off she spread her legs as wide as the could go. She heard some rustling around and yet with the blindfold she couldn't tell what he was doing. Her imagination ran wild and she let out a squeal when she felt a cool liquid hit her puckered hole. Lube. He was putting wet, cold and thick lube on her and rubbing it into her small rosebud. Preparing her.

"Ahh, what a flawless ass you have." She couldn't tell if he was talking to her or talking to himself. So she stayed silent. The press of his fingers into her ass almost sent her into overload; thankfully, she controlled her breathing and forced herself to stay focused.

"That's it, chica, take my fingers." He wiggled his fingers just inside of her rectum, stretching her to accommodate those appendages.

"Now let go of the covers and cup your breasts. I want to see you play with the nipples."

She groaned as she did what he wanted, cupping her breasts and tugging at the nipples with her fingers. Her breathing sped up and she pushed her ass into his fingers, taking both deep inside to the knuckle.

"You like this, don't you?" He chuckled.

She nodded her head.

"Speak, Aurora, or I will stop."

"Yes, Amo, I like it. More, please." She'd resorted to begging. "Please, can I see you?" She wanted to see him, her tormentor.

"No. You're not ready to see me."

She frowned. "What do you mean I'm not ready, señor? I'm more than set."

"Si, you are prepared for the anal plug, Aurora. As for the other, you think you're ready? That is for when I say you are and not before. Don't stop touching yourself. Keep touching those stunning breasts for me."

Her nipples were nice and hard from her torturing them and she bit her bottom lip, holding back the wail she could sense on the surface of her lips on the verge of bursting free.

Chapter Four

Felipe finally had her where he wanted her. She was on display and needy for only him. It had taken her long enough, he thought. It had taken a lot to get to this point. He would leave nothing to chance. He undid the tie of his white robe and tossed it to the side. He was naked beneath it.

"Tonight, Cielo is for you. I'm going to give you everything your heart, mind and body desires, for truly your wish is my command."

He reached for the anal plug that he'd put next to her on the bed and made sure it was well oiled with the lube. Once done with that he set the plug against her ass and though she wouldn't be able to make eye contact with him he looked down into her face.

"Everything, Amo?" Her breathing had sped up and he could tell she was doing all that she could to stay in control. He would break her of that. Her control was his control.

"Yes, everything, Aurora. Now I'm about to give you the anal plug. Once I insert it, you keep it in no matter what's going on. Do you understand?"

She nodded her head furiously and then bit out, "Yes, señor."

He pushed the plug into her. Since she'd already been prepared by his fingers the plug slipped in easily and without barrier. She uttered a deep moan. He settled back on his knees to observe his handy work as he wiped his hands with the hand wipes he'd placed next to her on the bed. *Damn, she was perfection incarnate.*

Her clit was distended and puffy and she was gushing her cream like no one's business. The hard tips of her chocolate nipples beckoned his mouth. She was a vision and he was a man dying of thirst. He arched over her, hands on both sides of her body as he bent his head to lick at one nipple and then the other. She purred softly. The sound of that purr made his cock ache.

"Is that how you ask for more, Cielo?"

"Amo, please give me more."

"Give you more of what, chica?" He tugged at her nipple with his teeth.

"That," she said.

He could see the pulse beating in her throat and then she swallowed hard, continuing what she was saying.

"I want more of your hands and your mouth on me. I want your cock inside of me. I need to come hard."

"I plan to make you come all night long. Don't worry."

"I can't help but worry, señor. It's been so long since I've come at the hands of a man."

Leaning in once more he trailed kisses along her neck and down between her breasts. She arched gently against his mouth.

"You have to trust that I will give you what you need, Aurora. This means you have to let go of the control you love so much."

"It's hard."

"Yes, it is. Once you let go, you will have all your heart desires."

Her background was the reason for her reluctance to give over to him. It had angered him before, and the ensuing fight had pushed her away from him. This time it would be different. She obviously wanted to submit. It was in her makeup. The tattoo was another indication that she hadn't truly let go of her past. The fact she'd put down on the forms she filled out her desire to be dominated said it all. Though her submission would be for him alone, he'd make sure of that.

"We will stop if you get too uncomfortable with what is happening. Now tell me out loud the safe word that you have picked." He of course knew the word. It was a word ingrained in his psyche. She'd used it before over eight years ago. He hoped he would never hear it from her lips again.

"Briar. I choose the word briar, Amo."

"So now we have your safe word, you will use it when and if you feel uncomfortable with anything and need to stop."

"I will use it if I need to, Amo."

"Now that we have that established, we will go back to our pleasure."

He cupped both of her breasts and pushed them up and together, licking gently at both buds of flesh. She had gorgeous breasts, nice and full. Enough to fill his hands generously and he had nice big hands.

She placed her hands on his thighs and he stopped his licking.

"Move your hands, Aurora. No touching until I say so." He would blow his load if she continued to touch him. Up until now she'd behaved and it had made it easier for him not to focus on his raging hard on.

His plan involved her first orgasm and then he'd let her see who he was. Then the true test would begin. Right now she thought this was just about her getting over her block with having a man touch her and orgasming. It was about that, but it was also so much more. He was going to push her boundaries to the limit.

First things first, giving her a little taste of what he had in store for her by giving her orgasm after orgasm.

"Are you're ready, Cariño?"

"Yes, Amo, I'm ready for anything you want to do to me."

He moved off of her body and back between her spread thighs. Placing his face just above her pussy he blew gently down on her clit and she squirmed. "Mmm, you're so ready to be taken. Your juices are coating the pillow." He took two fingers and placed them at her entrance and settled his mouth over clit, sucking it gently into his mouth.

"Oh!"

Flattening his tongue against her, he stroked it slowly over and over again and thrust his fingers into her deeply. It was time to give her a taste of what could and would be. Curling his fingers up towards her g-spot he rubbed them gently over that bump of flesh. Her sounds of pleasure soon turned to deep moans.

Taking his mouth from her, he said, "Come for me, Cielo, now."

He felt her body tense and then she was rocking and riding his fingers hard like there was no tomorrow. In the next moment she gushed her liquid cream and came in a heated rush. She drenched his fingers and lips she came so hard. The fabric below him was soaked as well.

"Amo Felipe!" she cried out.

"That's it, Aurora, seek your pleasure and take it."

He couldn't help the grin that crossed his face; she'd called him Master Felipe. That had to mean something. He lapped at the liquid that oozed from her pussy like a man starving. He'd missed this, missed her. When her body had finally stopped trembling he removed his mouth from her and sat back on his haunches.

"Oh god, you did it. You made me come."

"I promised you that and so much more. Are you ready to continue?"

"Yes, señor, I am. Please give me more. I want more."

"You beg so prettily, my dear. I'm going to use cuffs on you. Can you handle me taking away your freedom of movement?"

"I can take it, Amo." Her chest was still rising and falling quickly. He could see that it was her eagerness pushing her on. He got up from the bed and made his way to the nightstand. Opening it, he grabbed the handcuffs that sat within that drawer. He took the arm closest to him and put the cuff on it and pinned her to the headboard. He performed the same treatment on the other hand. Her eyes would be sensitive after being covered for so long. He didn't want her to be in pain.

"Do you realize what you called me?" Felipe wanted her to take in the fact that she'd called him by his name.

"I called you Amo."

"That's not all you called me, Aurora." There it was, the proof that she was still going to avoid that she needed him.

"What do you mean?"

"You called me Felipe."

"Well, yes, this is my fantasy. I can call you that."

"You're right. This is your fantasy." Relaxing back on the bed between her legs he stared down at his beauty. Enough was enough. Time for her to face her past and he was just the one to thrust her into her future fast.

"It's time to awaken, beauty."

As he said those words he removed her blindfold and tossed it on to the bed. He gazed down at her and watched as she opened her eyes slowly, staring directly at him, then blinked. Recognition came slowly, but it was there just the same.

NIKKI PRINCE

Chapter Five

"Felipe..." she whispered softly. The first thought that entered her head was that it really was him and it wasn't a dream. The second thought was, *oh my lord, it really is him*! Nervously she wiggled her hands in the cuffs, testing their strength. How did they find Felipe? Hell, for that matter, how had he found her? He hadn't aged a day. He still had that luxuriously long black hair, dark goatee and smooth olive complexion. The only new item on his body was the tribal dragon tattoo with a rose in its wings.

"Yes, Aurora, it's me."

"Let me go."

"No. You have not fulfilled your fantasy."

She struggled against the cuffs again. Closing her eyes, she tried to calm herself. She could feel her heart rate rising and she let go of a deep breath in an effort to find clarity. She wasn't trying to hear that he wasn't going to let her go.

"You made me come; you've helped me achieve my fantasy," she argued, trying not to look him in the eyes.

"Damn you, look at me." The tone of his voice forced her to face him.

"What is it you want from me, Felipe? You've proven your point that you can make me come where no other man has ever been able to. What more do you want?"

The expression that came over his face gave her pause.

"What is it that I've always asked from you, Cielo?"

"You're asking for something I can't give you."

He frowned and she sighed. "No, it isn't that you can't give it to me. It's that you're being stubborn and refuse to give it to me."

"Felipe, please just let me go. I don't want a repeat of eight years ago."

Felipe growled and moved off the bed. "You gave into me willingly just moments before. How can you deny how I make you feel? I am your fucking fantasy."

"Because we don't work!" She was lying to herself and to him, but she wasn't about to let him know that.

He laughed and shook his head. "We work very well together. I'm the master you've been waiting for. I'm the reason you aren't satisfied with anyone else. Now, you're paying for a fantasy so how about we fulfill it and if you're still not happy when our time is up, I will let you walk away."

"My god, you are still as cocky as all fucking get out!"

"Cocky and telling the absolute truth. You're so scared you can't even admit that I'm right."

"Felipe … we don't mesh." God, why did he have to look so good and make her body sing with pleasure? She didn't even sound convincing to herself.

"We more than mesh, Aurora. I touch you, and you melt. You cried out my name when you came earlier. Are you going to lie to me and tell me that meant nothing?"

"No. I won't lie to you about that. I did call your name out, and I did write that you were my fantasy lover. The keyword here is fantasy, Felipe."

"Prove it, Aurora."

"Prove what, Felipe?" She eyed him suspiciously.

"Prove to me that what we have is just a fantasy and I will let you walk away when the contract we have here is satisfied."

She turned her face from him and sighed, closing her eyes. It hurt to think that she'd be walking away from him; it would be for the best. Turning her head back she spoke. "Okay, so what are the terms?"

"They are the same as the ones you signed up for when you came here. I will give you as many orgasms as I can in our time together. You will relinquish your control and let me take over. I will show you what you've needed and been missing all this time since we've been apart."

What if he was right? What if she let go and let him show her what could be? What did she have to lose if she just let him have his way and she let go? Her heart. On the other hand, in reality she'd lost that to him a long time ago and without him she was only half alive.

"Okay, Amo. Show me what I've been missing all this time. If in the end it doesn't work out, you have to let me go."

"The full time, Aurora, and if you're not happy then I will let you go."

"Agreed."

"That means that anything I have planned you must go along with it. Unless it is against your boundaries, and then you are still required to use the safe word."

She nodded her head. "Yes, anything you have planned. I agree to you not stopping unless I use my safe word."

"I'm going to release you from the cuffs. Then I will be taking you out into the club. Think you can handle it out there?"

She eyed him suspiciously. "Taking me out into the club how?"

The grin that he gave her was enough to confirm that she should be suspicious. "Just as you are, naked and mine."

She was about to protest and then she saw the smirk on his face. The challenge in his eyes spurring her on, she'd prove to him that she could do this and walk away once more.

"Have you eaten?" he asked her.

"No, I was too—" She paused.

"Too what, Aurora?"

"Too excited about what would be happening tonight." The smile that spread across his face more than told her he was pleased with her words. She didn't want to admit even to herself that she loved to please him.

"The possibilities of what can and will happen tonight are endless, Cielo." He strode forward, stopping next to her, and undid the cuffs, tossing them onto the nightstand near the bed. She did not move, waiting for him to tell her that it was okay.

"What if this doesn't work, señor?"

He cupped her cheek and brought her face up to his. "What if it does, Aurora? It's time to stop running and face our destiny head on. You're not the only one that suffered when we were apart from each other. Now let's go and get you something to eat. Trust me to be able to give you all that you need." When he pulled up, he held out his hand for her to grab.

Trust. That was the big key. If she thought about it she'd always trusted him. It was herself she had a problem trusting. She placed her hand in his, allowing him to help her up and out of the bed. With the anal plug in she had to be careful so as to not make it come out. He'd told her she couldn't until he told her she could.

She moaned softly as her moving caused the plug to lodge even deeper within her.

"Ah yes, you still have the anal plug in. Good girl." His approval warmed her. That was one thing about him she was happy with. He always complimented her on doing what he requested of her. "So that means I have to carry you to our table." He pulled her flush against his body, and god, what a great body he had. His arousal would have been apparent to her, as it was pressing into her stomach as he held her.

"I still smell like sex."

He chuckled. "I'm sure that isn't a major factor here at this particular club. Besides I love that other men won't get to touch what's mine unless I say they can. You, my dear, smell heavenly."

"Amo Felipe. You haven't come. Let me take care of that for you." She pointed to his cock, which was pressed into her stomach as she faced him.

His eyes simmered with lust and without words he sat in the chair that was closest to them and cupped his cock. "Do you yearn to taste me, Aurora?" She followed the movement of his hand along his thick shaft. There was nothing hotter than a man masturbating. Well, other than that man masturbating for her.

Walking towards him, she placed herself between his thighs and nodded. "It's been a long time since I've had your cock in me. Seeing as you wish to torture me and make me wait before you fuck me, I'd love to have you in my mouth."

"Then work your magic, girl. Take some of the edge off." He pointed his cock towards her.

"Eagerly, señor." He was long and thick and the hair neatly trimmed there. That was one of the things she liked about him. He was one sexy man, muscled abs and all. She stroked her hand over his stomach and heard his sharp intake of breath. It thrilled her even more to know that just her touch got him excited.

Bending down towards his cock, she flicked her tongue around the head, and then teased it along the slit to lick the pre-cum pooled there. She ran the tip of her tongue around the head of his cock over and over again.

"Stop the teasing, Aurora. Take all of my cock and suck me off so I can go and show you off." Felipe had thrust one of his hands into her hair and tugged her down towards his cock. His other hand was still on his cock so that he was directing both of their movements. Sucking him into her mouth she didn't stop until he hit the back of her throat and her lips hit the top of his hand. With each of his thrusts into her mouth she hummed, using the vibrations to add to his pleasure.

Using a free hand she cupped his balls, holding them tightly to his body. She remembered he loved a strong grip. His grunt was the sign that she was on the right track. She squeezed gently, and he arched into her mouth and hands. Using her longest finger she rubbed his perineum. Rubbing back and forth gently over that small bundle of nerves to heighten his pleasure, she watched as his head fell back against the chair and his eyes closed. He kept a fist full of her hair as he thrust into her mouth at a quicker pace.

"Cristo, I'm in heaven. It won't be long before I fucking spill in your mouth."

Felipe took over and began fucking her mouth hard. His balls drew up towards his body and she recognized it as a sign that he was about to explode. The next warning she got was the hiss that escaped his lips and then his cream shot into her mouth. She drank hungrily, not letting a drop escape. Aurora continued sucking even when there was no more of his cream filling her mouth and she only stopped when he tapped her cheek gently. He withdrew from her mouth and she couldn't stop herself from taking one last teasing lick to the head of his cock. He growled softly.

His dark eyes glazed with lust, his long black hair in disarray about his shoulders as he panted. "As always, my dear, you continue to outdo yourself. That was exquisite. Now that you've taken the edge off, I'm going to take you out to our table and feed you. You ready to be on display?"

She licked her lips suggestively and winked. "I'm more than ready, señor." She didn't add that she wanted to experience everything he had to offer her so that she could keep the memories with her forever. No, she was going to continue with this fairy tale until the last possible moment.

Before she could even think to protest he had her in his arms and carried her to the door. He wouldn't have taken no for an answer besides, because he was her master and his rule was law. Least it was for now. Quickly she wrapped her arms around his neck, holding on for dear life. She allowed herself to relax against him, and giving up that little bit of control actually felt wonderful.

He was so strong and capable. From the moment she'd first met him at the lifestyle party she'd been drawn to him. She would make the most of the time she had with him here, because soon enough it would all be gone and she'd have to go about her life without him.

"Open the door, chica." She grabbed the doorknob and turned it, opening the door.

He kissed the top of her head and uttered his thanks as he stepped out with her in his arms.

NIKKI PRINCE

Chapter Six

If the club had been busy before, it was in full swing now. The dance floors lit up with lights as the clothed and the unclothed writhed to the beat the DJ played. Felipe moved through the crowd of people with ease, like a man who owned the place. The others parted and made a path for him, making her chuckle.

"Even here you seem to have a commanding presence."

"Others just know authority when they see it. Here we are." She expected him to put her down in the other chair, but no, he kept her in his lap.

"Not going to let me sit in the other chair?"

"No, Aurora. I want you in my lap so I can do whatever my heart desires to you. You're mine for as long as you're here."

His cock was nestled between her ass cheeks and was still semi-hard. Damn, she wanted to be riding his thick rod but until he said she could have it, she'd have to suffer. Their waiter came to the table with menus and placed them down in front of them. She couldn't stop the little giggle that escaped as she looked at the costume he wore. Fairy wings with boxers and as she looked around she noted that the female waitresses wore bikinis with fairy wings as well. Over their nipples the women wore shooting star pasties.

"Hello, Prince Felipe, is there anything you'd like to drink for you and Princess Aurora?"

Wow, they really take all of this very seriously.

"Yes, Sam. Bring me your best whiskey and the Princess will have the white wine." Sam bowed his head and moved off to get their order.

"You remembered." It was all she said. It amazed her that after all this time he remembered everything she liked. From being blindfolded to the wine she liked.

"How could I forget what you like?"

"Most men would, señor."

"I'm not most men and I think it would be best if you remembered that. Most men would not have done everything they could to find you again." Felipe leaned in and kissed her bare shoulder as he cupped both of her breasts in his palms.

With a soft huff she laid her head back on his shoulder, enjoying the roughness of his hands against her aching nipples. She wanted him again; it was obvious from her body's reaction. Fresh cream coated her inner thighs and soon would be dripping onto his lap.

"Mmm that's it, give in to me." He nipped where her shoulder and neck met and she moaned.

"Aren't you supposed to be feeding me?"

"Still hungry after what you did to me in the room?"

She laughed. "Mhmm, for food right now though. You I'm sure will give me just what I need after we eat."

She didn't realize that she'd closed her eyes until his words spoken softly into her air startled her.

"Sleepy, Aurora?"

"Not at all, señor. I was just relaxing."

"We have an audience already. Look to your left at the gentleman sitting on the couch." She turned her head in the direction he spoke of and sure enough there was an auburn haired male sitting on the couch with his cock in his hand, stroking at a leisurely pace.

"He wants you, Aurora. But you see you're mine and no one else can have you unless I give them permission. I'm going to invite him over but not yet. I want him to want you so badly it won't take anything for him to spill his load." Felipe nipped her ear and she groaned out loud. The images he was arousing in her were almost too much.

"You called me a tease earlier, but I think you're the tease, Amo."

"Yes, because two can play at that game, Aurora."

She shivered as he nuzzled her neck, licking at the skin there, and then giving her a soft love bite. "Is this a game, Amo?"

"You tell me, Cielo. Is this a game or something more for you?"

She started to speak then closed her mouth trying to think of the words to say. She heard him chuckle.

"It's okay; I will allow you to think about your answer. You can tell me at the end of our assignation."

It was best she stayed quiet. She'd take the time he'd given her and wait to tell him what he wanted to know. Right now though she'd enjoy that her fantasy come true held her breasts in his hands and had his shaft nestled snuggly against her ass while another man watched them. She adored being watched, one more thing about her that her master recalled. There was a bit of anxiety that she couldn't allow to rise, anxiety that she might lose herself by giving up so much power.

"Tell me, Aurora, what you'd let him to do you, if I gave you free rein."

The waiter returned with their drinks, setting them down before them so Aurora didn't say anything. The pinch to her nipple made her gasp, but not in pain. In fact, it just turned her on more. He knew how to give her just enough pain to exhilarate her pleasure.

"Come now, Cielo. I asked you to tell me what you'd let him do."

"Amo, you know I have not been able to come by another man's hand."

Another pinch was given to the opposite nipple and she mewled, rocking into his lap.

"That's not what I asked. I asked what you'd let him do to you. I didn't ask whether or not he could make you come. Besides, we both know that when you're with me another touching you gives you pleasure. It's only when I am absent that it stops." The waiter still stood patiently by the table.

"Amo, I'd let him suck my nipples, as it seems to be where his eyes are drawn."

"I don't blame him. You have beautiful breasts. You are perfection incarnate, mi vida." He placed a soft kiss to her neck. "Now it's time to feed you. We will have something light, Cariño." Felipe had always had names for her, and she didn't mind them one bit and would answer to them all. Tonight would be no different.

To the waiter he said, "Sam, we are ready for the Empanada Gallega, the pork version, along with some strawberries that I ordered."

Sam smiled and gave a bow of his head and walked off towards the kitchen, she assumed.

"You've thought of everything, Amo Felipe."

"It won't take any time for them to bring out our food. This perhaps is a good thing, seeing as our friend over there looks to be getting a bit impatient waiting for permission to come and sit over here with us. What do you say, Aurora, should I let him come sit at our table?"

"Only to sit, Amo Felipe?"

"Yes, only to sit for the moment. I still don't know if I will allow him to touch you."

"Amo, I only want your touch tonight."

"This isn't totally about what you want, Cielo. This is about you leaving your control behind and submitting fully to me." He took one hand from a breast and cupped her chin, turning her face to his.

"I want all of you or nothing, Aurora. Don't you understand that by now?"

His gaze was intense and she fought the compulsion to close her eyes. If she let him he'd devour her very soul. She shivered and he kissed the back of her neck as if to soothe her fears. If only that would help, she'd know what to do and what would be happening by the end of the evening that didn't involve her running away. *Running is the only option. Not yet. Enjoy this time, as it will be all you have with him.*

For the first time that night she felt like crying, but she couldn't do that in front of him so she blinked back the tears. Something flickered in his eyes, and she couldn't begin to describe what it was.

"Our food is here … we will eat and then it is time for some serious play." He let go of her chin and she saw Sam placing the food down with two small plates.

"Drink if it helps calm your nerves." Felipe picked up his whiskey and sipped it. For a moment she watched him, even waited to see him swallow. Everything he did was so fucking corporeal and sexy.

Zealously she picked up the wine and took a sip, almost choking herself in her eagerness. She set it down quickly as she coughed.

"I said to calm your nerves, not choke yourself, Aurora. Don't rush."

"I was a bit too fast, Amo Felipe." Sheepishly she glanced up at him and couldn't resist the urge she had to kiss him, so she did just that. A quick kiss to the corner of his mouth and then another.

"Mmm and what brought those about?" he inquired.

"I couldn't help myself. I love your lips, so sensual."

"As I said before, don't rush." His head descended and he took her lips in a heated kiss, tasting and savoring her as if she were that fine wine. He licked at her lips then sought entrance, thrusting his tongue into her mouth, and she tasted his whiskey and the flavor that was uniquely him. He teased his tongue along her teeth then swirled it around hers before sucking it into his mouth.

She whimpered in his mouth when all of a sudden her head was pulled back as he tangled his fingers into her hair. This action thrust her breasts out and arched her throat. She was completely at his mercy.

The lick and nip to her throat was a surprise to her. It could only mean that Felipe had given permission to their observer to touch her. Felipe kept kissing her even as the other man made his home at her throat. It was intoxicating to be worshipped not only by the man you wanted but to also have another do so at that man's request.

With a soft growl Felipe parted the kiss, tugging at her bottom lip with his even white teeth, then licking over the small bite. She stayed like that, staring up at him, seeking his guidance.

"She is wonderful, eh, Nico?"

"Si, she is, just as you said she'd be."

Her eyes opened. He knew the other man? Why not? Everything seemed to be part of his plan anyway. Besides, he was giving her everything she wanted. True, she'd put down what she wished for, but some things she hadn't even been mentioned and yet he'd provided them. She might as well just hang on for the ride. Literally and figuratively.

Chapter Seven

"Take a seat, Nicolai. Eat with us, then you can come back with us to our suite."

Felipe let go of her hair after one hard kiss to her lips.

"Eat now, Aurora."

She was so horny all she wanted to do was get fucked. Then again to disobey her master was a no-no. She turned to the food and began to eat. The empanada was delicious and melted in her mouth. The two men conversed while she ate and the ensuing camaraderie comforted her. Felipe only wanted what was best for her. She was a submissive: he was a dominant. The love she'd felt for him scared her. She wasn't the type of person to just give a bit of herself when she found love; no, it was all or nothing. When she'd had her fill she pushed her plate away and picked up her wine, taking a small sip and settling back into Felipe's arms. The men continued to talk a few moments longer and then Felipe finally spoke to her.

"Go back to the room, my beauty. Nico and I will follow you shortly."

She nodded and scooted off his lap quickly. She took it as him giving her space and time to come to grips with what would be happening once they were all behind closed doors. Walking back to the room, her eyes feasted on couples and groups of people in various stages of flirtation to full on sex. There were men and women wearing the collars of their masters, those who loved the schoolgirl look to the straight on leather or latex look. Anything could be found here, it seemed, from vanilla to whatever was your flavor.

She stopped to watch as a Domme strapped her male sub to a Saint Andrew's Cross with bondage cuffs.

He was completely naked and bound with the intricate Kinbaku knots in a vivid blood red that caught her eye, and she couldn't look away. Kinbaku was basically what the western culture called Shibari. The Domme asked her sub if he could move or get away, and she heard him tell his mistress that he couldn't and that he'd gladly give up all for her, even if she spurned him.

Aurora's heart constricted at the thought of giving all over to Felipe and him telling her at some later date he was done with her. No, she wouldn't do that with him. She'd never give him that pleasure to just up and leave. She'd be the one to do the leaving. Frantically she looked over in the direction where Felipe sat with Nico. Noting they were still there, she made up her mind in that moment.

It was now or never. She backed up, choosing now, almost knocking over Sam the waiter to rush back to her room. He grabbed her to steady her. She made her apologies and ran towards the room as if Satan were on her heels. She was leaving, and this time would be the last time he'd ever see her. No matter how much she loved him, and in that moment she knew she loved him, she wasn't going to be left to pine for him.

To let go completely meant that she'd be losing herself. There would be no identity left for Aurora Devine. Her mother had given all she could to her father only to have him pick and choose when he'd spend time with their family. Each time he came back her mother got weaker and weaker, saying it was for the best and that she loved her husband. Her mother, once a proud and beautiful woman, became a husk of her former self, taking what little scraps she was offered.

She'd be damned if she'd grovel at a man's feet, no matter how much she yearned to be his and how good it made her feel; she couldn't in her mother's memory allow it. No, in fact she wouldn't allow it. Her mother had died a broken woman pining for a man who didn't want her. Felipe called to that part in her that desired to submit. However, the other part of her loved her freedom and was afraid there would come a time when she was no longer wanted. No longer the pretty woman on Felipe's arm but an object that dulled in comparison to the next female that caught his eye. It would crush her to see him turn from her, to no longer wish for her to be his. In as much as a submissive was her master's, a master was the submissive's. It worked both ways. She'd just have to go on for the rest of her life with the memories of him and fuck having an orgasm by the hand of another man.

By the time she made it to her room her heart was racing and tears were streaming down her face. The first place she headed to was the bathroom. She slipped the plug out, cleaned it, washed herself up and then headed back into the bedroom. Thrusting the door open she went straight to the closet and took out her clothes. She was so busy trying to put on her clothing she didn't hear the door open and close.

She was in the midst of slipping on her panties when Felipe spoke up. "Where do you think you're going, Aurora?"

Christ, I should have put the panties in my pocket and not taken the extra time to put the damn things on. Freezing briefly, she realized she was holding her breath and released it on a soft huff.

"I'm leaving, Felipe." She didn't bother to call him master, because she was leaving. She could only guess that waiter Sam had seen her fleeing and had spoken to Felipe.

The normally cool, calm and collected Felipe's nostrils were flared. He was angry. *Let him be angry.*

"What changed your mind, Aurora? When you were at the table with me you were fine and now you wish to leave?"

"I decided that what you have to offer isn't what I want." She swallowed the bile that filled her mouth. She was making herself sick with that lie. She had to make him believe it, so that he'd let her go.

"Put your clothes back in the closet, now."

She frowned and squared her shoulders. "You have no right to tell me what to do, Felipe."

"I have every right, Cielo. You gave me the right to tell you anything when you agreed to staying here and fulfill the contract."

"I changed my mind." She defied him and continued to dress, her eyes trained on him for any sudden moves so that she'd be able to counter them. Hopefully.

"Now you sound like a little girl who's lost her dolly." His words dripped with sarcasm.

Moving forward as if she were brave she stopped in front of him.

"Please move, Felipe. I need to go. I've wasted enough of my time here. I'm sorry I can't do this any longer. We don't fit."

"That's a matter of opinion, Aurora. We fit very well and have from the beginning. I'm going to ask you one more time to do as I ask and then I'm going to show you how wrong you are." He barred her from the door and in frustration she made as if she were going to move past him and gasped as he grasped her wrist and spun her around so that she faced him and her back was to the door. He took her other wrist in hand and brought them up above her head, holding them against the door.

"Joder, you'd try the patience of a fucking saint, Aurora!"

"You're no saint, Felipe!"

"Something you'd best remember, Aurora." Felipe growled out. His face was inches from hers and her heart was in her throat as she struggled against him to no avail. She was no match for his strength. Though he wasn't hurting her he was making it impossible for her to go anywhere.

She whimpered softly and squeezed her thighs together. *How could she want to smack him one moment and in the next moment want to fuck him until they were both raw?* He knew exactly which buttons to push to make her putty in his very capable hands.

"Aurora, I can smell how much you want my cock in you. Why are you denying what we both want?"

"Just because you want something, doesn't mean it's a good thing, Felipe."

"Grow up, Aurora. I'm your dream, your fantasy. Be a big girl and reach out and grab it."

"Felipe..."

"Tell me to let you go, Cielo. Tell me you don't want my hands on you and you don't want what I have to offer. Let it be the truth and I will let you go."

She trembled against him and his eyes sparkled deviously. "Tell me..." His voice was hypnotic. "Convince me that you want to be free from me."

Every bit of his naked body touched her in some way and his heat seeped through her clothing.

"Felipe, please..."

"Please what, Aurora? Please let you go? Please fuck you? Which?" He nuzzled her neck, and she groaned as his goatee stroked along her skin there. God, why couldn't she walk away like she had before?

"I want to give you what your heart's desires, Aurora. Why won't you let me?"

"For how long, Felipe? How long before you tire of me?"

He pulled away from her neck, frowning. "What the hell are you talking about? I've always wanted you and I've never tired of you."

She started crying again. Why did he have to sound so convincing and trustworthy? "You'll tire of me Felipe, and then where would I be?"

Felipe let go of her hands and cupped her face gently. Leaning in he kissed her eyes and then licked at the trail of tears that flowed down her cheeks. When he got to her mouth he kissed her deeply. The urgency in that kiss made her soften towards him, and she cupped the back of his head, threading her fingers through his thick ebony strands. He took that as his cue to take what he wanted, and boy, did he. With quick movements he divested her of her clothing again, tossing each article to the floor.

"You're mine and you will stay mine, Aurora."

She was tired of arguing with him about it so she didn't say anything. He was correct—she was his, and she'd always been his. She was just iffy on the matter of him being hers. She was too scared to ask him. She was also filled with so much hunger for him at the moment the thought of questioning something she feared hearing the answer for wasn't an option.

Chapter Eight

He'd be damned if he'd let her go. He wanted her, had always wanted her and she was here within his grasp. She didn't want to leave him. Something had scared her and he needed to figure it out. She had to know that he'd do anything to keep her safe, anything. He longed to take care of her, give her everything she needed

He picked her up and carried her over to the bed, setting her down on it. "I want you, Aurora. I'm going to take you. The question for you is do you want me to do that without Nico present or with him present." He was going to keep to her fantasy.

"Bring him in, Amo." She sounded breathless.

"Are you sure, Aurora? Nico being here is part of your fantasy. So are you telling me you still wish to participate in that?"

"I want it. I want to experience that with you, if only for this moment." He watched as she lay back on the bed. The sexual need was obvious as she writhed on the bed, small moans slipping past tight lips.

"This is the second time that you've disobeyed me, Aurora. As your master I'm beholden to giving you punishment. First, you took out the plug, and second, you were about to run out and leave me high and dry yet again. Any punishment I give you would be something you'd like. I fear that everything I do to you would be something you want. Am I right?"

"Right, and now I want it all," she whined.

"Lay there, don't touch yourself. I forbid it." Turning from her he picked up the telephone on the nightstand and dialed a number.

"Send in Nico with the items that I requested, please." He hung up the phone and grabbed one of the condoms that sat on top of the nightstand. He opened the foil wrapper and held out the condom to Aurora.

"Come here and put this one me, beauty."

She scrambled off the bed and grabbed the condom, kneeling at his feet. Damn, she was gorgeous. There was a knock at the door, and Nico entered the room carrying the requested items. His attention returned to Aurora when she took his cock in hand and glided the condom on.

Once she was done he held his hand out to her for her to stand. Cupping her gorgeous chocolate tipped breasts in his hands he leaned close, licking around each nipple in turn.

"Such beautiful breasts. Don't you think so, Nico?"

"Fabulous breasts, Felipe. I wholeheartedly agree." Pushing his hands up under her breasts as if checking the weight of each he grinned as Aurora began panting.

"Ah, beauty, you love your nipples to be touched. I say a bit of clamping is in order, what about you?"

She let out a ragged moan and nodded her head. "Yes please, Amo."

"I'm going to take it one step further. I'll give you the nipple clamps, and I'm also going to add a little surprise."

Her eyes widened and he could tell she wanted to know everything that would be done to her. "Not going to tell you right now, beauty. As you can see our wonderful friend and observer Nico has set up the bondage swing. So I'll ask you to go and get nice and comfortable in the swing. I don't want you on your stomach. I want you to see everything that's going to happen to you."

While he'd been talking to Aurora, Nico had quickly assembled the swing in the middle of the large room. Nico took her to the swing and got her settled then both of their gazes turned to Felipe. That made him smile. It was proof he was running the show.

"You look as good as I knew you would in that swing, beauty." The swing was in all black, padded for her comfort with back and butt support and with straps for her feet. Nico adjusted the straps so that it fit her body impeccably. She was a vision. Her pussy glistened with her juices and he wanted to lap up her nectar as well as plunge into her again to make her his. Soon.

"Thank you, Amo."

"Do you have the clamps I asked for, Nico?"

"Of course, right here. I've been dreaming of seeing these on her."

Nico held up a silver set of c-shaped nipple clamps to him, and Felipe strode over, taking them from him.

"Thank you," Felipe said.

Pinching the handle open to one, he set it against her left nipple and then closed it around it. She gave a sharp hiss and then he saw her bite her bottom lip and wiggle in the swing. "How's that feel, Cielo?"

"Oh god I love it, señor." She moaned out arching upwards.

"Mmm, good. Now for the next one." He added the other to her right breast and observed her have pretty much the same reaction as before.

"Ohhhh!" She cried out and bucked in the swing.

"You've been asleep way too long, my sweet. It is time you were awoken by your master's kiss. Do you understand the difference between becoming a slave and being a submissive?"

"I...I..." He watched his mocha beauty struggle for a few seconds and then held his hand up.

"It doesn't make you weak to wish to submit in all things to me. You're a strong woman. I'd be a weak man if all I wanted was for you to be my slave. When you submit to me, you do so willingly and voluntarily. Your pleasure is my pleasure and vice versa."

Nico brought over a red Japanese drip candle, and Felipe took it, holding it up to Aurora.

"You know what this is, right?"

She nodded her head frantically, and he saw her bite her bottom lip.

"This is one of the little added surprises that I promised." With those words he placed the candle up over her chest and let the wax drip down and onto her skin. She muttered his name on a long, drawn out sound. Each drop of the wax was hitting her lovely skin, and she purred every time the wax trickled down onto her.

"My, my, my, you're so responsive." He dribbled more wax over the other breast and again observed her reaction. He did this several more times until she had a pattern of wax streaking over her chest and down towards her stomach. The last bit of wax dripped onto her clit, and he watched as she bucked hard in the swing.

She was spread so openly to him that he could see her muscles clench and unclench as she writhed in pleasure. He grabbed the bottle of lube Nico had set on the floor next to the swing and squirted it out onto her ass. She loved having her ass played with and he wasn't about to miss the opportunity to give her everything she required.

"It's time to take care of her ache, Nico. Take the candle and go ahead and have a seat. I can't wait any longer. Hell, I don't think any of us can wait any longer."

On cue Nico was next to him, taking the candle and handing him a dildo. Double penetration, she had marked that down as one of the things she wanted to experience. It was long, thick and curved. He held up the dildo, showing it to her and smiled as she licked her lips. "This is for you, Aurora. Pleasure beyond anything that you can imagine, that is what I will give you. No longer will you sleep."

Pressing the dildo to her ass, her body took it hungrily and quite easily since she'd been prepared for it. His face level with her pussy, he leaned forward to lick at her.

***

It was almost too much; with the clamps, the wax, the thick dildo, Nico watching and Felipe licking her she almost came. She bit back the next cry as he rolled his tongue against her distended clit and teased it. Her head fell back, and she focused her eyes on the ceiling. Something she hadn't noticed was that the ceiling was covered in mirrors. She could see everything.

"Mirrors," she whispered softly.

"Yes, mirrors so that you can enjoy every aspect from every angle."

"Ohhh, Amo ... please more. I need you."

"Who do you need, Aurora?"

"You, I need you!"

The words tumbled forth and she couldn't stop them. It was obvious from how wet she was in the first place. His words ignited something in her that she couldn't contain. He loved it when she told him what she wanted.

"That's my girl. Tell me what you want and how you want it."

"I want you in me, hard and fast. Fucking me so hard you make my teeth chatter."

She heard a groan off to the side and saw Nico with his thick cock in his hand pumping eagerly as he held his balls in the other hand. He'd even dribbled some of the wax onto his own chest and all over his cock. The sight sent a shockwave of burning hot need through Aurora. She loved to watch too and wasn't ashamed of that fact. Everyone's pleasure in the room mattered.

"Do you like that, Aurora? Like that Nico is so hard he is about to burst. He wants to fuck you, he can't and he knows it. Makes it that much more delicious to him, having the knowledge that he can't touch unless I say he can."

"I love it. I love knowing that he wants me but I'm yours to command and to take."

Felipe wrapped his lips around her clit, applying hard suction. She rocked back and forth in the swing, fucking his face. Felipe detached his mouth from her clit then stood. Her eyes met his in the mirror and she cried out as he slapped her clit with his cock. The sting caused from that action radiated throughout her body, and she gripped the straps of the swing in expectation of what he'd do next. The one thing she loved about him was that he was always unpredictable. Her needs always came first and he seemed to anticipate them before she did.

"Yes, you're mine to take, mine to fuck. Mine, Aurora, do you hear me?"

She thought about what he'd said. It was true her pleasure was his and his was hers. In the time that they'd been together in the past he'd never done anything to hurt her. All that she could ever dream of was given to her.

"Yes, Amo, I'm yours, completely and irrevocably yours."

"That's what I wanted to hear from you." He placed one hand on her waist, the other at his cock, and pressed deep, so deep she could swear he hit her cervix.

The room was filled with the sounds of moans as Felipe, her master, thrust into her at a leisurely pace.

"Fuck, Felipe, you two make a gorgeous pair." This came from Nico, who was leisurely stroking his cock from base to tip as he eyed them both nonchalantly, so relaxed.

"Mmm, si, we do, Nico."

Felipe growled and sped up, his thrust hitting so hard the smacking of his balls against her body could be heard echoing through the room.

It had been so long since she'd been fucked like this. His thick shaft filled her so completely. Each thrust drug him along her inner walls, which clenched to keep him within her. She was close to coming. Her body began to tremble, and he tightened his hands on her waist, grinding into her.

"Oh god, Amo, I'm so close!"

"Hold it, my sweet, and I promise you the longest and hardest orgasm yet."

God, what a promise and if anyone could deliver it would be her master. She groaned as the chain from her nipple clamps received a tug and it was then she realized that her eyes were closed. Upon opening them, her gaze met Nico's as he stood over her, his cock in one hand and the other holding the chain. She'd hold it and come when Felipe allowed and not before.

"Señor?" she questioned lightly. She had to make sure that Nico wasn't doing anything he shouldn't.

"Si, Aurora, it's okay. Nico knows the boundaries. You and I talked about having him taste your beautiful breasts. You still okay with that, my beauty?"

Breathlessly she said, "Yes, Amo, your pleasure is my pleasure, remember?"

The spark that lit his dark eyes thrilled her and the grin that spread across his countenance was even better.

"Si, this is for our pleasure. Let us continue, Aurora."

NIKKI PRINCE

Chapter Nine

"Nico, release Aurora's breasts from the clamps and then you can have a taste."

"With pleasure, Felipe."

Aurora let out a small gasp as one clamp was released and then the other. The feeling rushed back into her breasts. The pain was exquisite torture. The heated coolness of Nico's mouth on a nipple had her arching up into him hard.

"Ohhmmm…" she moaned.

"I think she likes that, Nico."

Fuck, that was an understatement. She clenched around Felipe's cock, her pussy beginning to contract as she neared another hard come. There was a tug at her clit. Her master it had to be, as Nico was only allowed to taste her breasts. Felipe used his fingers to pull and pinch slightly and she let out a long wail as she came hard on Felipe's cock.

"I think you're right, Felipe. Your girl does like it. How lucky you both are." Nico tugged on the chain as her master fucked her smoothly. The dildo added another level of pleasure as Felipe fucked her. It pressed against the thin membrane of skin inside of her, and she started trembling. She was lost, but she had to hold on for her master's command.

"Joder! Come for me, corazón, come hard!"

Felipe cried out and bucked against her harder and faster, pushing her further and further into orgasmic bliss. Vaguely she heard Nico cry out, and she knew he was coming by his own hand though his mouth stayed on her nipple sucking so hard it was like they were part of each other. There was no beginning or end to this. Everything just melded into one, and she couldn't hold back the sob as tears poured down her face.

He'd done what he'd promised, given her the pleasure she sought. If she stayed with him there would be more. But it wasn't just about the sex. No, Felipe made her feel loved and cared for. She sensed that deeply in her heart of hearts.

When Felipe pulled out of her, she felt bereft. Next to go was the dildo, and she groaned, unable to stop the tears that flowed. She hadn't had closeness like this in such a long stretch. Aurora heard moving around but didn't open her eyes, and then she was being cleansed with warm cloths. Instinctually she knew that both men were cleaning her. What a perfect way to end such an incredible moment in time.

Sobbing quietly to herself as her body calmed, she didn't resist as Felipe gathered her in his arms and removed her from the swing. She buried her face against his neck and held on tightly.

"Shhh, mi Amor, let me take care of your every need. I have you," he whispered softly in her ear.

His words immediately calmed her and it was as if the past eight years had never happened. He carried her to the bed and settled there with her. Nothing was said and the only sound was the opening and closing of the door marking Nico's exit. For a long while he held her, just rubbing his hand over her back gently and kissing the top of her head.

"Now do you see that we're meant to be?"

"I see it. I see it as clear as day. I was scared, Amo."

"I know you were, Aurora, which is why I gave you the space you needed. Till your mind caught up with what your body and your heart wanted. Tell me your fear."

"I feared that you would leave me high and dry as my father did my mother. I didn't want to be like her…"

"What I've told you stands true. This isn't just about what I want. I don't want a slave; I've never wanted a slave. What I do want is to take care of you in all ways. You yearn to submit, I yearn for your submission. As for me leaving you? Never. You are my life. If at any time you wish to go, then you would be the one leaving. My heart and soul are forever entwined with yours."

She turned her face to look up into his eyes. "Amo … I'm sorry to have wasted so much time."

"No, don't be. It's what we needed. A break, time to figure out what we wanted. The time wasn't right, and now it is."

"The fears will take a while to go away," she cautioned. "I've held on to them for so long. I know you're not like my father."

"Yes, they will. I will be with you every step of the way. You are my light in this world. I love you. You're right; I'm not him and will never be like him."

"I love you too. I always have." He leaned down and kissed her lips softly. She kissed him back, pouring all of her emotions into that kiss. When his lips parted from hers she cupped his cheek.

"You're still the beautiful strong woman that you always were. I wouldn't ever want a puppet on a string. Your submissiveness calls to my dominance, and we fit perfectly. The dragon tattoo that I have on my shoulder, I got it the day you left. For me it is a symbol of me protecting you. My Briar Rose, my sweet love."

She brought her fingers to his tattoo and traced it gingerly. It was true he'd always been her protector, the one man she could count on to give her what she needed mentally and physically.

"How did you find me?" She wanted to know.

"The night you left me I'd just been returning home. I saw you fleeing and followed. I've never been far behind, my sweet. As I said, you needed space and I gave it to you. I found out that you wanted to have a fantasy come true, and I just made sure I was the one signed on to give it to you. Doc Fairee and I go way back. Do you believe in magic?"

"Magic, Amo?"

"Si, magic, mi vida."

She grinned widely and nodded. "Yes, I believe in magic. It was magic that brought you into my life in the first place and it was magic that kept you in my life. You call me your heaven, your life, your dear, your love and your heart. I think that about sums up the magic in my life."

"Ah, you've brushed up on your Spanish." He chuckled.

"Of course, I had to make sure I knew exactly what my Latin master was calling me." She winked at him.

"I've been calling you terms of endearment, my girl, all terms of endearment." Leaning up, she kissed him softly.

"I give it all over to you, señor."

"I take it all gladly and with pride. You will have everything your heart desires and even if you wish to work that isn't something I will take away."

"My job is very demanding. What I would like to do is to scale back a bit and focus on being yours." She gave a small yawn and snuggled close. "We still have four days here."

"The club is actually mine so we have as much time as we need and then some. Dr. Fairee didn't want to let you in on the fact that I owned this place. It would have messed up the fantasy. I made sure that he has been paid handsomely."

"He's getting paid by you as well?"

"No, all the money that you've paid to him was put into an account for you. I'm paying the good doctor."

"So you've been taking care of me all this time..."

"I have and will continue to do so. I make enough money with the family business so that you don't have to work. Although if you wish to be a modern woman and work, who am I to deny you that? Between the wineries and the wish business, you and I can live quite comfortably. The one thing people never tire of is sex and alcohol."

"Oh you're right about that, Amo. So what's next?" She wasn't ever going to tire of having sex with him, that was for sure.

"Sleep for you and then we shall make both our wishes come true over and over again."

"My wish came true the moment you had me blindfold myself and sit in the middle of the bed."

He laughed. "Hmm, that reminds me you have a punishment coming."

She grinned. "Oh yes, I do."

"You, my Cariño, seem to love your punishment a bit too much."

"It's because you give out such punishment so deliciously."

"Mi vida es mágica contigo en ella."

"My life is magic with you in it too, Amo."

They snuggled close together in the bed, and she knew that all would be okay. She'd come home to her master, and though it would be a step-by-step process, things would work out for the best, because their love was all the stronger.

NIKKI PRINCE

CINDA'S FELLA

DEDICATION

There are a few steadfast friends who helped me immensely while writing this book. Piper Anderson, Kim McNiel, Michelle Carnes, Doris O'Conner, Shyla Colt and Melanie Fletcher. Thank you ladies. It's always a pleasure to be able to bounce ideas off of you all and to know that we all have each others back.

NIKKI PRINCE

CINDA'S FELLA

Once Upon a Dream, 2

Nikki Prince

Copyright © 2013

Chapter One

Cinda Augustine Rella sighed as she looked down the long deserted hallway in the office building that she had the task of cleaning. A building she'd have to clean in high heels no less. She'd have to take them off in order to move around and get things done fast. She didn't want to run into the owner of the building. She wouldn't be there if her normal janitor hadn't called off sick.

It was Thursday night and instead of enjoying herself she was here cleaning. Such was her life. This was an important account, and she had to make sure that it got done while Jaq was off. She didn't have anyone else yet who could do it, so being the professional she was she'd do it herself.

Hopefully the owner of said building wouldn't be around. She'd spent too many years trying to avoid him and stay professional. Nicolai Charming made it hard for her to be good. He was damn sexy and a redhead to boot. She adored redheads. Nicolai was his own set of trouble. When she was around him there wasn't a moment that went by when she didn't want to strip naked and do anything he asked of her. She sighed and closed her eyes as she remembered his touch. There was nothing that compared to Nico's touch.

He'd been the perfect sensual Dom to her submissive tendencies. He gave her anything she could ever want. Then her stepsisters and stepmother had happened. Drusilla and Anastasia had been the bane of her existence since they'd come into her life. Their mother, who made Cinda call her Ms. Trumane even after she married Cinda's father, had made things just as hard as her daughters had.

Her father, God rest his soul, had married their mother when they were teens and life had never been quite right since. Within weeks of finding out her father was dying from cancer, he and his second wife died in a car accident. She'd thought she'd be free of the two sisters once and for all and be able to grieve for her father in peace.

No such luck. Unbeknownst to her, her stepmother had cajoled her father into changing his will and having the sisters and their mother added to it. Upon her stepmother's death whatever part was given to the stepmother reverted to her daughters. Her father's cleaning chain was what was up for dibs. She'd received half of the business in the will and the two sisters had received their share along with dividing their mothers share between them. Thus, the two sisters together had half of the business and did basically nothing for it.

Her father's cleaning business had been his life. He'd built it from the ground up on his own, and she intended to keep it going for him. It wasn't a business that had board members in charge, but it did well. She planned to keep it that way. She wiped away the tears that had escaped and then squaring her shoulders she bent down and took off the silver heels she'd worn with jeans and the company t-shirt. She'd had no time to change when she'd found out on short notice that Jaq would not be working tonight. One thing she loved was her heels, and she'd wear them with anything if she could.

Setting the shoes on top of the cleaning cart, she then pushed it into the last office she needed to clean that night. It was Nicolai's. Flicking on the lights in the room, she noted that he still had recessed lighting. It enabled her to see, though the room was still cast in shadows in some areas. The last time she'd been in his office had ended with them at odds with one another. She had to block out what happened, as it was the only way to get her work done. Soon she was caught up in cleaning his office window that she didn't notice she wasn't the only one in the room until she heard the clearing of a throat.

Jumping, she turned around slowly to see who it was. Recognition hit her full force as she looked into Nicolai's green eyes. She was mesmerized and she could only utter a small squeak in place of words. She watched as the lazy grin spread across his face and he stayed settled at his desk. God, how had she not noticed him? Her mind had been on other things—that was the only explanation.

She finally found her voice. "Nico, what are you doing here?"

He laughed and she flushed. *What a stupid question.* "Hmm, well, this is my office, Cinda."

"Yes, right. I guess I meant why're you here so late. But then that would bring up the same answer. You can be here as much as you'd like. I was just cleaning; I can go and come back when you're gone. My regular janitor for your offices isn't here." She was rambling. He stood and with a gasp she hurried towards the door. Her only thought was of escaping.

"Going so soon, Cin? We haven't seen each other in years." He was barring her way. She stopped just in front of him.

"There's a reason for that, Nico." She licked her lips and groaned inwardly as his gaze riveted to her mouth and his grin widened even more.

"Now, now ... you know you don't mean that. I know you so very well, like the back of my own hand, Cin."

He was right, he knew her, though that didn't mean they needed to be together in any way, shape, or form. He advanced and she moved back. She held her hands up to stop him from getting any closer; he pressed his chest into her hands, and she discerned it was on purpose.

"Master..." The word was out before she could stop it.

"There, now tell me that doesn't feel right. Tell me."

She didn't say anything, just continued to stare up into the most gorgeous eyes ever. She swallowed hard.

"You can't tell me because it wouldn't be true." When he cupped her chin in his hand, she let go the ragged breath she'd been holding. His touch sent electricity through her body. He was always so gentle and caring, something she hadn't had in her life before him or since.

"Tell me that you don't want this ... me."

She couldn't tell him that, because it wouldn't be the truth. She'd wanted him from the moment she'd met him. He used the pad of his thumb to stroke over her bottom lip and when she didn't move away he moved his thumb and replaced it with his lips. She moaned, her hands still against his chest, but curled into his dress shirt.

He tugged at her lips with his teeth then teased along the seam with his tongue, demanding entrance. Unable to deny him anything she parted her mouth and moaned softly as his tongue filled her mouth.

He drew her even closer when he hooked his fingers into the belt loops on her jeans and tugged her forward. The evidence of his desire pressed against her lower belly through his pants. She didn't resist him. In fact, she whimpered when he parted the kiss.

"Damn, I've missed your taste, girl."

She licked her lips again and his gaze darkened.

"You know just what to do to me."

As he said those words he walked her backwards and then she felt the desk bump the back of her legs. She opened her mouth to protest and it was as if he knew that's what she was going to do as he covered her mouth with his own.

Besides their breathing, the only sound in the room was the rasp of her zipper as he undid her denims then pulled them down over her hips. They pooled at her feet and he picked her up and settled her on the edge of the desk, causing her jeans to slip off and onto the floor. She was in a pair of silk bikini panties and a t-shirt that was emblazoned with her business name, Midnight Cleaners.

He drug his mouth from hers. "This is your last chance to say no…" He was gently massaging her back. He'd always had strong, capable hands that turned her to putty.

"Please…"

"Please what, Cin? It hasn't been that long that you don't know who I am to you." He pulled her t-shirt up over her head, tossing it to the floor. When he cupped her breasts and kneaded them, she arched into his hands. She cried out as he nipped the tops of her breasts.

"Who am I to you, Cin?" he said once more, a bit firmer than before.

"Master Nico..."

"That's my girl." She shivered as he all but purred those words to her. She felt her pussy dampen even more and she squirmed against him. He made her forget herself.

When he knelt before her, settling between her spread legs, all she could do was watch. Eye contact with him was always a must and a requirement.

He grabbed her bare feet, gently caressing them both, kissing the toes on one foot, then the other. She groaned but stayed perfectly still.

"Ah, you know I adore your feet. Next time keep the heels on."

She couldn't let there be a next time, but she wasn't going to tell him that. She'd let him get comfortable and when he didn't expect it, she'd run. She had to.

He kissed his way up her leg then draped that leg on his shoulder. He gave the same treatment to her other leg. With both legs on his shoulders, she was as open to him as she could get without him taking off her panties.

"Please, Master Nico."

He seemed riveted on her panties and when he spoke she knew why.

"Damn, you've soaked through your panties and I haven't really touched you."

"You've always done that to me."

"Pull your panties to the side. I'm going to taste you. Open yourself for me."

Without hesitation she brought her hand to her panties and pulled them to one side. Glancing down she could see the hood of her clit, which was stiff and throbbing. She could also feel her juices coating her inner thighs.

"Fuck, girl. You've kept yourself shaved as I requested."

She wanted to deny what he said, but it was the truth. There wasn't a lick of pubic hair on her, as she'd shaved herself bare. She'd kept herself up to the specifications that he'd demanded from her even though they hadn't been together in years. He leaned in close and took in a big breath, as if he was trying to breathe her in, and she held in a lungful of air in anticipation.

With the first swipe of his tongue she bucked against his mouth. He peered up at her and instinctively she recognized that meant for her to relax and practice her breathing. He didn't want her to come yet. It would be a struggle, as it had been so long, but she didn't want to disappoint him. She'd never wanted to disappoint him. She had though when she'd run.

"Pure honeyed excellence. You taste just as sweet as I remember."

She braced herself on his desk because she knew him well enough to know what would come next. The nip to her inner left thigh made her squirm with delight.

"You've missed this just as I have, Cin. When are you going to recognize that and stop running?"

Once again she was pinned by his stare. The one thing about Nico was that he seemed so calm and for the most part he was. Yet at the same time there was that inner strength he exuded, showing he was a master through and through.

"My life…"

"Is incomplete without you, Master Nico." He finished for her.

Nico was right; her life was incomplete without him. But dealing with her stepsisters and the business was a full-time job. She didn't have room for him even if she wanted it. She started to protest, and he shook his head, placing his finger against her lips.

"No, we aren't going to discuss that right now. Right now you're going to come for me because you need it and I want to see it."

He spread her legs wide, propping them on his desk so that she was bared to him. Obediently, she kept herself exposed with her hand still holding her panties.

"Every day that I've been in this office, I've thought of you. Taking you here and watching you cry out your pleasure. We'll make new memories for the both of us."

He dipped his head between her thighs and licked her roughly. She bit her bottom lip to hold back the moan that was just on the edge of escaping.

Chapter Two

He had her right where he wanted her. He could feel the resistance leaving her. He couldn't let her leave him again. Enough was enough. This was where she belonged, with him. He'd do anything to get that through her head, even have her employee call in sick. He'd have to thank Jaq for agreeing to do so.

He wrapped his mouth around her clit and rolled his tongue around it. Feeling her tense, he knew she was fighting the urge to come. She was his good girl. Even after five years of being apart, she still followed his commands. Fuck, he couldn't resist her taste. Lifting from her once again he locked his eyes with hers.

"Tell me what you want." He knew what she wanted. Always. It was his job to know what she needed and to give it to her.

"Master Nico, please allow your girl to come. I need to come hard on your mouth and tongue."

"If I allow you to come, you must promise me that you'll meet me at the club."

He watched as her eyes closed and she let out a soft sob. She would know exactly what he was asking of her. If she came to the club, she'd be his and he'd be her Master once more. Nico wouldn't give her time to ponder what he was asking. Letting her think about it could backfire. He smacked his hand against her clit and she jerked, her eyes opening quickly.

"What's your answer, Cin?"

He saw the war of emotions go across her face and just when he thought she'd bolt she nodded her head and spoke.

"Please let me come, Master, and I'll meet you at the club whenever you like."

He thrust two fingers into her pussy, going knuckles deep and then stopping. As wet as she was, he went in nice and easy. Her pussy hungrily swallowed up his fingers. His eyes never leaving hers, he watched as she squirmed.

"You're right. You'll meet me whenever and wherever I say. Fuck my fingers, Cinda. Fuck them until you come nice and hard. I want to see you fucking squirt."

She rose slowly and thrust herself down on his fingers over and over again until she was moaning with each upward and downward stroke. Her beautiful brunette tresses had fallen out of the ponytail she'd been wearing and fell down her back. Her head fell backwards and soon she was moaning his name over and over again. The closer she got to coming the raspier her voice sounded.

"That's my girl. I can feel your pussy clutching my fingers. You will come but only when I let you come."

Leaning forward he kissed her at the juncture between her stomach and her leg, nipping at the skin as she finger fucked herself. He wanted to fuck her. But he'd save that for the club. Their joining would be special. He'd make sure of it.

Standing, he thrust his free hand into her hair and tugged until her head fell back. Curling his fingers inside of her till he hit that small bump of flesh inside of her, he stilled her actions. She was panting heavily, her breasts rising and falling quickly as he watched her struggle to not come. Her breasts were damp with the evidence of her exertions.

"I'm going to let you come, Cin. As soon as I rub against your g-spot let go and give it all to me."

"Yes, Master Nico." She was breathless.

He smiled and pushed both fingers against her special spot and watched as her body began to buck uncontrollably on his desk, showing she was overcome with desire. The first bit of fluid from her pussy leaked around his fingers and pooled out of her and then she was gushing liquid as she cried out. Not one to leave her hanging and give her the female version of blue balls he pushed down on her clit and rubbed as she continued to orgasm. The amount of liquid that came out of her was amazing in its copiousness, and he was well and truly soaked. He took her mouth in a hard kiss, swallowing her cries. He kissed her through her orgasm until she was whimpering and shivering against him.

Slowly he removed his fingers from her then lifted them to his mouth. He had to taste her again, so he placed both fingers in his mouth and licked them clean. Damn. She was all he'd thought about for the past five years. He gathered her up in his arms and carried her over to the couch in a corner of his office and held her close. Her breathing was still ragged. He would let her catch her breath then they had some talking to do.

The moment her fight came back he knew it and he held her as she tried to get out of his lap.

"Where do you think you're going?" He placed a kiss on top of her head.

"I need to go. I shouldn't be here, and I shouldn't have promised to meet you at the club."

"Ah, but you are and you did and the Cinda I remember would never renege on something she's promised." He felt her shoulders sag, and she lay back against him. He stroked his fingers along her back, content just to hold her, though he knew that they truly did need to talk. When she squirmed once more, he placed a hand under her chin and tugged till she looked up at him.

"Why did you run from me?"

"I couldn't stay. There was so much going on at home."

"Yes, your father died. You wouldn't let me comfort you."

She shuddered, and he saw the tears forming in her eyes at the mention of her father.

"Please don't make me talk about him right now."

"If not with me, who will you talk to about this? You have to talk to someone."

He stroked the pad of his thumb slowly along her chin. She was so soft; he could not help but touch her in some way.

"I'm okay. I can get through this. I don't need to talk to anyone."

"Really? Then tell me why are you crying and why you continue to run from me if you have it all under control?"

"We aren't meant to be."

He laughed and she looked at him, a frown on her face.

"What's so funny?" She still had that adorable grimace on her countenance as she asked him that question.

"We connect on so many levels. You need me just as much as I need you. Why won't you let go and let me take care of you?"

"I don't need to be taken care of..." She sobbed and he held on to her even tighter, comforting her.

"Yes, you do. You above all others need to be taken care. You've spent all your life taking care of others. You took care of your father, who was terminally ill, your stepmother and your two stepsisters." She gasped and he nodded. "You didn't think I knew that, did you?

Those very sisters you're still taking care of and don't have to, Cinda."

"Dad had cancer." She began to cry. "I promised him that I'd take care of everyone. I couldn't. I ... just couldn't disobey him."

"Shhh ... it's enough for right now. You don't have to tell it all to me in one sitting." He rocked her gently back and forth, rubbing his hands soothingly over her back.

She wiped furiously at the tears streaking down her face. "How did you know I'd be here?"

"Truth is, Cin, I had Jaq call in sick."

"Why would he do that?" She was looking up at him with her big caramel-colored eyes. Cinda was so beautiful and so his.

"He did it to get us together at my request."

"You talked to Jaq about us?"

"Yes, I talked to him about our being in a relationship. I didn't say anything about our lifestyle together, but he saw the picture that I have of you over on my desk and a conversation started one day. He just happened to mention that the woman in the photo looked like his boss."

She glanced over at his desk. It was apparent she couldn't see the picture he was speaking of when she turned back to him.

"Which picture?" she whispered softly.

"The first one we took together, our first date."

"The one we took at the amusement park." It wasn't a question, but a statement of fact, and it showed she remembered. She swallowed hard and pressed her forehead to his.

"That very one."

He could describe the picture by heart if she'd asked him to. She'd been smiling as they stood in front of a fairy tale castle, his arms around her as he stood behind her and they both peered at the camera. She'd told him she'd wanted to feel carefree as she had before her mother had died and her father had turned to the other woman in his life. So he'd taken her to the amusement park.

"I need to go." She had her face pressed to his throat and as she spoke her breath tickled across his skin. He was as horny as a man could possibly be, but years of discipline held him back from taking her just yet. They had some issues to get over within their relationship. The main thing was that Cinda needed to give over her trust completely. If she didn't, it would destroy the both of them. He couldn't go another five years without her, and he was sure she wouldn't be able to as well.

Chapter Three

The look of determination in Nico's eyes more than told her that he wasn't going to take no for an answer.

"The only place you're going to go is from here to my bed, Cinda. I don't want to let you go. I'm tired of waiting for you to figure out that your place is with me."

"I can't just drop everything. I have responsibilities."

"You mean you have Drusilla and Anastasia to take care of? They're old enough now to take care of themselves. Instead of just leaching off you and the business your father built."

"Please, I don't want to argue about this anymore."

"Then come with me for the weekend. Meet me at the club this Friday night. If after this weekend you no longer wish to be in my presence, I will honor that."

What could a weekend hurt? She'd get to spend a few more days with the man she'd loved for the last five years and then when the time came to leave him, she'd at least have the memories to hold on to.

"I can't think with you holding me this close. Please just let me get dressed so I can think."

He let her go, though it seemed reluctantly, and she stood. Grabbing her clothes from the floor, she dressed slowly. That was when the fear crept in yet again. She couldn't do this. There was too much at stake. She glanced back at Nico who sat on the sofa as relaxed as a tiger ready to pounce on its prey, drenched in the evidence of her need for him. There wasn't a man in this world more beautiful or dangerous to her. From his closely cropped red hair and perfectly groomed red goatee to his 6'4" muscled body, he was it for her. It was a shame she couldn't indulge and let him keep her. Her mind made up, she gave him a smile that she was sure conveyed her sadness and regret and just as he stood she bolted. This time she made it out of the door but not before grabbing her heels and running.

She was almost out of the building when she dropped one of her heels. Looking behind her she gasped as he was almost on her. Turning she left the heel and opened the office door, running with her bare feet and not stopping till she made it to her car. She pushed the button that would open her keyless car and got in, starting the vehicle and peeling out of the parking lot at the stroke of midnight. The last thing she saw in her rearview mirror was Nico standing in the parking lot with her silver shoe in his hand and a dark glare on his face, watching her drive off. Once again she'd let her Master down. She let the tears fall.

***

Disappointment had washed over him as he watched her drive off and out of his life once again. Reaching into his pants pocket he pulled out his cell and dialed. Placing the phone to his ear he waited for the recipient of his call to answer. It was time to call in the big dogs and he knew just who to get ahold of.

"Doctor Fairee, how can I help you?"

"Wonderful, you're in; I was thinking I'd have to leave a message."

"Nico, my boy, what can I assist you with?"

"I need help capturing my own wish." He'd spent a lot of time helping others make their wishes and fantasies come true. Now it was his turn to be on the receiving end.

"Let me guess, dear boy, you want to get Cinda Rella back into your life to stay." The good doctor had been instrumental in helping him find Cinda the first time. Nicolai had been coming to the club for years with no true connection to anyone other than Felipe. Doctor Fairee had suggested that he speak with Cinda, as they seemed to have personalities that would match, amongst other things. Boy, had he been right.

"Yes, that's what I want. I had her here tonight, but she's run again. I don't think she and I can take much more time alone."

"It's my job to make wishes come true. I'm sure I can come up with some satisfying way to bring about your very own dream come true."

"Yes, you did a wonderful job with Felipe and Aurora."

"My dear, dear boy, that wasn't all me. You played a huge part in it as well."

"That may be, but this time … I'm in need of your help. If you can just get Cin to the club I'll do everything else."

"I'll get her there." He heard the older man chuckle. "After all it's what I do."

"And you do it so well, my friend. Thank you."

"No thanks are needed, you know that but you're welcome. Make sure you fill out the forms for all the things you want to have happen."

"Yep, I know the drill … consider it done." He hung up the cell and dialed one more number.

"Felipe."

"Hey, man, sorry to disturb you. I'm going to request one of your suites for this weekend." He could hear some giggling in the background and he recognized the laughter as coming from Aurora.

"Shh, mi vida," he heard Felipe say. There was another soft giggle and then silence. "Of course, anything for you, my club is open to you at any time. I'm sure you've already spoken with Fairee to have him work his magic?"

"Si, I called him before calling you. I appreciate this, bro."

"Think nothing of it. You know mi casa es tu casa."

"Mm, yes I know. Still though, I'd rather ask you out of respect. Thank you, my friend. I hope you and Aurora will be about this weekend?" Felipe and Nicolai had been friends since college. Both men having the same tendencies towards kink they'd shared women from time to time. So when Felipe had come to Nicolai to ask for his help in making his dream of having Aurora come true he'd done so.

"Hell yes, we wouldn't miss it for the world."

"Excellent, see you there." He was about to hang up when Felipe spoke up.

"You okay, mi amigo?"

"No, not really, but I will be. I just need her back in my life. I know you feel me on that."

"Si, I totally understand. If anyone can work miracles and get her there, it will be the Doc. You'll just have to get her to stay."

"Therein lies the rub, Felipe. I will be pulling out all the stops to keep her. Once she's there I'm not going to play fair."

"I don't blame you. Whoever said all in love was fair was wrong." They both chuckled.

"Let me let you get back to your Aurora. See you soon."

"Like I said before, wouldn't miss it for the world."

Nico hung up the phone and pocketed it and then headed back to his office with the sexy silver heel in hand.

***

The sound of her bedroom phone ringing pulled her out of her restless sleep and sent her scrambling to pick it up. She picked it up on the last ring.

"Hello."

"Is this Cinda A. Rella?" The voice sounded very official so she answered quickly, though she heard the question in her own speech as she waited for the male on the other end to speak again.

"Yes, this is she."

"This is Senior Officer Gus Octavius."

What the hell was an officer calling her for?

She sat up and settled back against the pillows and wiped her hand wearily over her eyes. She eyed the clock sitting on her nightstand and blinked. It was only eleven at night. She'd gone to bed early, having slept badly the night before.

"Okay, I don't mean to be rude, but am I supposed to know you?"

"Pardon me, ma'am, I didn't mean to imply that. I'm the head security guard at *Fantasy,* the exclusive club in the city."

Her frown deepened even further when the guard mentioned the club's name. *Fantasy.* It was the club where she was supposed to meet Nico. The club was her old stomping grounds, the place where all her fantasies and dreams had become a reality when she was with him. Every fantasy possible could be had there. *What a crappy coincidence.*

"Um, okay, again I don't mean to be rude but why is the head security guard for the club calling me? I don't remember owing anything from the last few times I visited. In fact it's been a few years since I've been there." The officer went on to tell her exactly why he was calling, and what he told her definitely made her wake up quickly. When she got off the phone she fell back against the pillows and covered her eyes with her hand.

Cinda grumbled to herself. The security guard Gus told her that her sisters were in custody for having ordered rounds of drinks and dinner, and then trying to skip out on paying the bill. He wanted her to come down so the two girls could be released. They'd given her name as the point of contact.

How'd Ana and Dru found out about it? Why were they there in the first place? God, the possibilities of what could be wrong were endless when it came to those two. They were queens of jealousy and troublemaking, and if there was a way to try to annoy Cinda, they'd find it. Boy, had they found it.

She'd rushed home after the incident with Nico the day before and now she had to trek down to the club to see what mischief they'd gotten into. When would they ever grow up? You'd think that with their mother's death they'd see that life was short and make changes, but sadly that hadn't happened.

The last thing security officer Gus told her was that she'd need to be in club attire. She wouldn't be allowed in if she came in street clothes. That was when she'd let out her frustration over the whole incident and yelled at the guard, stating that she knew the rules. She understood she'd have to be in club attire. Most specifically she needed to be in stilettos.

Annoyance burned through her. There was no way it didn't come across over the phone, which made security officer Gus restate his position.

"Ma'am, I understand your frustration. I'm only telling you what I was told to tell you. You will need to come here and speak with my boss once you do."

"You can't understand my frustration. Forgive my outburst, but there is no way you can understand. Tell your boss I will be there." She hung up the phone.

Boy, he was clueless. As many times as she'd been to Fantasy she had knowledge of the rules and what was expected. The place had a dress code to be sure, and she'd have to play by those rules in order to step foot into it. Shaking her head, she got up to shower and get dressed. This was turning out to be a hellish week.

So there she was dressed up as if she was going out for a night of fun in her car driving to the club in the hopes that she could get in and out without having to see Nicolai Charming. The club was his release. There was no doubt in her mind that he would be there. Now all she had to do was get in and get out.

NIKKI PRINCE

Chapter Four

Anastasia looked at Drusilla and scowled.

"You know, Cinda is going to be pissed, right?"

"When isn't she pissed at us?"

Anastasia couldn't help the laugh that tumbled forth. "When we're asleep?"

"Yeah, you got that right." Drusilla giggled and played with brown hair.

"She has to take care of us, has to." Anastasia shrugged her shoulders standing to pace back and forth in the security office they'd been left in. They hadn't seen anyone since being escorted in there and giving the guard Cinda's name and number.

"Well, it's not our fault we drank way more than we could pay for." Dru giggled.

"Well … damn right it isn't." Anastasia hiccupped and both women fell out in peals of laughter. "Although I think breaking the glass behind the bar we were at was a bit much. Nor was it cool to leave such a mess at our table. I think we may have messed up the stools. Hell, I don't remember all that we did." She shrugged her shoulders.

"I think we're just a lil' bit drunk." Drusilla snorted and they both laughed again.

"Nope, I think you're wrong, Dru, we're a lot drunk." Anastasia hiccupped several more times.

"So what are we gonna tell Cinduh?" Dru asked her. Anastasia giggled because they always exaggerated Cinda's name on purpose.

"We're gonna tell her to pay the bill."

Drusilla made a silly face at Anastasia, and they went into another fit of laughter.

***

Cinda pulled up to the club and parked. Closing her eyes for a moment, she focused on what she needed to do. Her plan of attack was to go in and get her sisters and then leave. There could be no other way around it. Turning off the car she stepped out and closed the door. She ran her hands over her body slowly to smooth down the red zipper dress she wore with the six-inch black stiletto heels. If she didn't have to be at the club to clean up someone else's mess, she would've actually enjoyed having to be all dolled up.

Before she changed her mind and left her sisters at the club to rot, she put one foot in front of the other and walked to gate where a man guarded the door with a clipboard. He had to be about 6'6" standing there in black. It was Lucien. No one messed with Luc. As big as he was he looked like he could crush a person's skull with his bare hands. As intimidating as he was, he was also handsome. With hair black as sin in a military cut and his wolfish good looks she was more than surprised he wasn't in the club having his own good time. From what she'd been told he'd been in the military before getting out and coming to work as a bouncer at the club.

"Hey, Cinda, long time no see." He smiled at her, his blue eyes twinkling.

"Luc, it has been a long time." She gave him a genuine grin. This was one person at the club that she didn't mind seeing. He leaned in and picked her up, giving her a bear hug. She squealed and wrapped her arms around his neck, kissing his cheek. He set her back down on her feet.

"You're looking mighty fine these days, girl. Where have you been hiding yourself?"

"Not necessarily hiding, but just not here."

"That's a vague answer. Though it's okay, I understand. Now go ahead on in. I'm sure everyone will be happy to see you."

She gave him a pat on the shoulder and moved past him. "Thank you, Lucien, I won't be in here long."

"Really? Nicolai is in there," he called after her just as the door closed. She froze in place as his words washed over her and left her shivering in their wake. She'd known he'd be there, and now the urgency she'd felt before came back. The club was teeming with occupants; it was the same as it ever was. The thrum of the music filled her with the urge to dance, to be in the scene again, but that wasn't what she was here for. She had to snap out of the lure of the club and keep to task.

Making her way to the desk she looked at the blonde behind the desk. Flora. She was another permanent fixture around the club that Cinda remembered very well. Flora glanced up from the paper she was looking at and recognition filled her eyes. The club was teeming with patrons in various states of undress.

"Cinda, it's a pleasure to see you again."

"Hi, Flora. It's good to see you too, but you must know I'm here to see your boss. Not here for a pleasure trip."

Flora nodded her head. "The boss is in his office. Follow Dante and he'll take you to him."

Cinda nodded her head and said her thanks and went willingly with Dante. They didn't have far to go before he stopped at a door, opened it and stood to the side for her to go in. She stepped inside.

She stopped just inside the door. Felipe Castro was sitting at his large desk with Nicolai Charming settled at the edge of his desk talking to him.

"Come on in, Cinda, and have a seat." Felipe spoke up first and pointed to the chair at the front of his desk.

"What is he doing here?" Her legs felt like jelly as she forced herself to get to the chair and sit. Crossing her legs she put her hands on her knees as she sat up straight. She had to keep her hands in her lap, so she could stop them from shaking. She watched as Nicolai smirked. He still didn't speak, and she tried to ignore that he was there.

"He's here because he's offered to pay the debt that your sisters built up if you agree to a contract with you as his sub."

Her breath caught. "How do you know that I can't pay it?"

"Let's see. They built up a tab so high that they can't pay it. Not to mention the damage that they did before they were escorted from the dining area." Felipe leaned forward, pushing a piece of paper toward her. She reached over and grabbed it. The number of zeros shocked her.

"Please, there has to be something I can do to make this right." Tears filled her eyes at the mess that was her sisters.

Nicolai picked that moment to speak. "The way to make it right is standing before you, Cinda. All you have to do is reach out and grab it."

She clenched her hands in her lap, looking down at her hands, as she didn't have the courage to look up at Nicolai in that moment. So instead she spoke to Felipe.

"Sir Felipe, is there no way to amend this other than me taking a contract with Sir Nico?"

"Truly there isn't any other way, Cinda. You've been a submissive to Nico in the past. Why is it a problem now? Has he abused you in some way that you didn't make known?"

"No, Sir Felipe, he hasn't. He was always the perfect Master to my being his slave." She couldn't lie. The truth was Nico had been wonderful in so many ways. He'd taken care of her and given her the things she yearned for. If anyone had been awful in the relationship, it had been her because she'd continued to run from him.

"This way the bill gets paid and your sisters won't face criminal prosecution for the all the damages and skipping out on the bill."

Cinda still refused to look up at them, keeping her eyes on the paper and her hands.

"Eyes on us, Cinda," Nico said softly, but there was that command behind his voice that had her doing what he said.

Felipe turned to Nico. "I'm going to go out and let you two figure this out. If she's agreeable then you will meet Aurora and I for drinks at our private table. That is, after Cinda has seen to her wayward and very drunk sisters." Felipe stood and nodded at Cinda then strode from the office, closing the door softly behind him.

"How were you able to accomplish this, Nico?" she whispered.

"Actually your sisters helped. They somehow managed to be their normal selves and found this club and the rest was history. Perhaps I owe them a bit of gratitude for this."

"This isn't a laughing matter."

"You're right, this isn't a laughing matter. What this is is you coming to your senses and taking what I can offer you."

"I have a lot at stake," she argued.

"This is all about trust. You need to learn to trust your own instincts as well as to trust me. You must learn to trust or you're going to be forever alone and cleaning up everyone else's messes. Now ... what will it be?"

Her options were slim, and she recognized that fact. It was either pick him or her sisters would wind up being in trouble with the law. Even if they weren't worth her protection she'd always do it. There were worse choices to make. She adored Nico. She just wasn't sure if they could work.

"What are the terms of the contract?"

"The terms would be I'd have you for the weekend and continuing the contract beyond that is negotiable. You'd be my submissive again here at the club for the weekend. This means as your Dom I can do anything I want within the limits you impose. It will be a D/s standard contract with a safe word if you choose to have one, Cinda. All of this will be just like we had in the past, nothing new, nothing shady and no surprises."

He held up a piece of paper and then handed it to her. Taking it from him, she noted it was indeed a contract with both of their names on it. She skimmed it quickly; there was nothing on it out of the usual. It stated that he'd pay all debts incurred by Anastasia and Drusilla as long as Cinda A. Rella became his submissive for the weekend. All neat and tidy.

He left his spot and moved to stand behind her. He placed his hands on her shoulders, gently massaging her. She hissed softly when she felt his lips nipping at her earlobe. She shuddered. His closeness made her wet and instantly needy. Her resistance, already at a low, was nonexistent as soon as he touched her.

"What's your answer, Cinda?" He placed a silver pen in front of her so that she could see it.

"Yes. I'll do it for the specified time of this weekend, Master Nico."

"Take the pen and sign. I'll sign after you. Then I will take you to your sisters and we will get them taken care of together."

She took the pen and with no hesitation she signed the contract. The last piece of the puzzle clicked into place as Nico signed as well.

NIKKI PRINCE

Chapter Five

"Come, we have to take care of your sisters and then it's time to go have some fun." He took the contract and pen and left them on Felipe's desk, then held his hand out for her. She took his offered hand, and standing, she slipped into his arms as he wrapped them tightly around her waist and held her snug against him.

"Give me your lips, Cinda."

She lifted her lips to his and let out a soft mewl as he covered her lips with his. He thrust his tongue into her mouth, licking and sucking at hers. He tugged at her bottom lip with his teeth, and then let go. She was well and thoroughly kissed by him. He cupped her ass and squeezed, and she purred, softly rubbing herself into his body. Nico slipped his hands under her dress, sliding his hands into her panties and cupping her naked ass cheeks into his palms.

"Master Nico..." She wanted more, and she was prepared to beg for it.

"Enough, we have plenty of time for this later. I'll give you everything you want then. Now let's go take care of your sisters."

***

Drusilla groaned as she was ripped from one of the best dreams she'd had in a while. Someone was shaking her shoulder.

"Stop it, Ana!" she groused.

"Dru, wake up. Cinda's here and with the sexiest man ever!"

Those words made Drusilla sit up, and she wiped the slobber that had come out of her mouth and dribbled onto the table with the back of her hand. Damn. Ana was right; the man was the sexiest ever. *What the hell was*

Cinda doing with him? It was very apparent that Cinda was with the man, as his arm was at her waist and he had her pulled as close to his side as possible without being indecent. Then the dreamy man spoke.

"Hello, ladies, I do hope your stay here has been pleasant as we could make it?"

"Um … um … um…" Ana stuttered and then yelled out 'ouch' as Drusilla elbowed her.

"It's been fine, 'cept a little longer than we would have liked," Drusilla countered.

"Well, you did destroy property and try to skip out on your bill. How did you two find out about this club?" Cinda said derisively.

"We were going through your mail. There was this golden card that had a silver shoe on it with this address." Drusilla couldn't stop the giggle that escaped. "So we decided this looked like a happening place to check out. Hell, you're all work and no play. So we were nosey."

Cinda was about to speak, and Drusilla saw the protective hand that Nico put up. Her eyes narrowed. *Interesting. Let's see how far I can get with this.*

"We figured you'd be able to pay for it, Cinda." Drusilla shrugged.

"You figured that you could come here and do what you want at your sister's expense?"

Hmm … Mr. Suave cared about Cinda and was very, very protective from the looks of it.

"Why not? It's the least she owes us after having to put up with her all these years. Our mother would be still alive if not for her father." She heard Cinda gasp, and her grin widened. *Take that, you privileged bitch.*

"So out of some misguided attempt to hurt Cinda you trashed my friend's club? Figuring that you'd be able to get away with it?"

"Yep, that's about the size of it. Who'd even have thought our Cinda was a closet freak. Into kinky shit and stuff," Drusilla informed him.

There was a knock on the door, and Mr. Handsome turned from them and went to answer it. She kept her eyes narrowed on Cinda, who had the audacity to have the sad look on her face. Her momma didn't raise any fools. She'd get what she could out of this and relish every bit of it. Cinda wasn't family, Anastasia was.

She watched as Cinda crossed her arms over her chest and stared her down. *Well, well ... our little miss is getting some balls.*

An older gentleman was ushered in and stopped to stand next to Cinda. The guy that had been with Cinda closed the door again and turned back to them.

"Hello, Doctor Fairee." *Ah, so the little mouse knew the newcomer. Curiouser and Curiouser.*

"Good evening, everyone, do forgive my lateness. I had a few things to peg down before coming."

What the hell did the old fart have to do with this? "And who are you?" Drusilla asked, giving Anastasia a sidelong glance and a shrug of her shoulders before she looked back at the man looking over his spectacles at some papers.

"I'm Doctor Godwin Aloysius Fairee. Drusilla and Anastasia Trumane, I presume?"

"Yeah, that's us. What of it?" *I swear I'm going to kick Ana's ass for playing the damn mute.*

Dr. Fairee moved forward and set the papers he was holding in front of them and pushed them forward so that they could see what they were. Scanning the papers quickly, Drusilla noted that it was the will that had been executed after her mother and stepfather had died.

"Okay and this is supposed to mean what to me and Ana?"

"It means exactly this, young lady. It's a fake. So we have a few ways that things can be done to work this out. I'm here to look out for Cinda's wellbeing."

"What do you mean it's a fake?" *What the hell was the old goat talking about?*

"I mean exactly what I said, it's a fake. Your mother, or someone your mother was acquainted with before her death, signed Mr. Rella's name to said document. I've had it analyzed by an expert. It isn't his signature."

All three women gasped.

When Drusilla recovered she could only gawk at the man.

"That can't be!" Dru argued. What he was saying meant that her mother had lied to her and Ana. Her mother had told them that she'd secured their future with Mr. Rella.

"Oh, but I assure you that it is. Now, what's going to happen is that you and your sister are going to leave quietly. You're also going to start doing your part with the cleaning business and will get a stipend. You will also turn over your part of the business to Cinda, as the business is rightfully hers."

"But … but..." Anastasia said. Finally, thought Drusilla, though what her sister had said didn't help one bit.

"My mother told us she'd secure our future!"

"Apparently she used subterfuge to do so. Now the other thing you will do is that you both will move out of the family home that belongs to Cinda and find your own place. I have all the documents here that you will sign to that effect. If you break any of the rules within these pages, you will be cut off completely."

"How do Ana and I know this isn't some trick?" Drusilla was going to stick to her guns. There was no way she was going to let Cinda win. No way in hell.

"Oh I assure you, my dear, dear girl, it isn't a trick. I figured that you and your beloved sister would need proof that it isn't a ploy. So, first thing in the morning, we have a meeting with a forensic document examiner. I know it's going to be Saturday morning but the examiner is willing to meet with us for a price, a price that I might add I'm willing to take care of."

"A fucking what? What the hell is a forensic document examiner?" Drusilla had had enough and she stood this time, facing off with Doctor Fairee.

The older man didn't flinch. In fact, there was a smile on his face.

"A forensic document examiner, my dear, is a person who verifies signatures and can recognize when something is a forgery."

"How the hell did you get the will in the first place?" Drusilla spouted off.

"Hey, you aren't going to pull a fast one on us. Why wouldn't the executor of the will know that the signature was fake if it was fake?" Drusilla gaped at Anastasia. It was the first intelligent thing she'd said all night. She'd stood now as well, placing her hands on her hips.

"Because, my dears, he was paid to be silent. So what will it be? When that little tidbit was found out and with him possibly going to prison, he sang like a song bird."

"We want to speak with the document examiner first. We aren't going to sign a damn thing till then."

"That's fine with me. Is that fine with you, Nico and Cinda?"

Cinda nodded and Nico spoke. "It's fine. Is there anything else you need from us right now, Doc?"

"No, not right now. I will call you tomorrow after our little meeting with Grandee Duke. He's expecting us at lunchtime. I figured there would be a bit of a snag with these two. After all, who'd want to give up the good life and using of another person?"

"Then Cinda and I will make our way out. We have a dinner date with Felipe and Aurora."

"Sounds great. You two run along, and I'll make sure that these two find their way out."

"This isn't over! Don't act as if we're invisible and not here!" Drusilla screamed at Cinda's and Nico's retreating from the room. She was still screaming when the door shut, and they were left in the room with the insufferable old man.

    ***

"Master Nico, how'd you ever accomplish that?" She couldn't help but ask him as he escorted her from the room.

"Doctor Fairee is a magical genius." He winked at her.

"Okay, well, I'm very curious as to how that little miracle was worked. I didn't know all this time that it was a forgery."

"Well, you wouldn't have any reason to believe that your father didn't sign it."

"True." She sighed. Was the servitude to her sisters finally over? Time would tell. She'd breathe easier once they signed the contract, but right now she wouldn't think of anything other than being in her master's arms.

"Now we will join Felipe and his beautiful Aurora for some drinks and perhaps something to eat."

"And then?" She received a smack to her ass, and she gulped. The sting from his smack sent a tingling sensation through her body.

"You're mine for this weekend and as mine you will not question what your Master has in store for you."

"Understood, Master Nico, please forgive your girl."

They'd stopped at a table and there sat Felipe with a gorgeous woman at his side. She could only assume this was the Aurora that Nico had mentioned. Nico held out a chair for her, and she slid into it and he settled next to her.

"Everything settled then, Nico?"

"Si, everything is perfect, mi amigo. Doctor Fairee has a way with making wishes come true."

"Cinda, this is my girl, Aurora." Cinda looked to Aurora and smiled as Felipe introduced them. "Aurora, my beauty, this Cinda A. Rella and you're well acquainted with Nico."

"It's a pleasure, Cinda." Aurora reached across the table to offer her hand and Cinda took it, shaking it.

"It's my pleasure as well, Aurora," Cinda said softly, looking from Aurora to Felipe then Nico. *God, what do they have planned?* She was nervous and excited. Nico alone was enough to make her worry about what was happening, but add in Felipe and his woman, there was no telling what was going to happen.

"It's time to have a drink and then we can all retire to the private suite," Nico said as he raised his hand and within an instant there was a server standing there.

"Bruno, we'll have some whiskey and Moscato Di Asti wine for the women."

"Of course, Mr. Nico, I'll bring that right away." Bruno was a tall man and not too shabby in looks either. Cinda remembered him well; he'd always been nice to her. If she remembered correctly as well that Luc had a thing for Bruno, she had to wonder how that was fairing. It had been so long. She'd have to ask Luc sometime.

Her train of thought was interrupted when Nico's hand slid up her dress under the table and gave her leg a small tap. It was the signal for her to open her legs. She bit off the moan that would have tumbled forth as he slipped his fingers into her panties and began to play with her clit. If the other two at the table had any inkling of what was happening, they didn't say anything. In fact, they seemed caught up in each other as well. Felipe had pulled Aurora into his lap.

Chapter Six

"Relax, Cinda." Nico leaned close and whispered in her ear, licking the lobe.

"I c-ca-can't, Master Nico," she said quietly.

"You can and you will, Cinda. I'm going to continue to touch you and you can't come. It's part of your punishment for running."

Her head fell back against the arm that he had resting on her chair. She bucked slightly as he dipped the tip of a finger into her entrance, swirling it around in her juices.

"Yes, Master Nico." She whimpered.

"Felipe has a wonderful idea." Before she could fully comprehend what he meant he'd removed his hand and picked her up and set her in his lap just like Aurora was in Felipe's lap.

She could feel his cock pressing into her ass as he established her on his lap. It was a deliciously sinful sensation. She rested back against him, leaning her head to the side as he kissed the side of her neck, nipping at the skin there.

He trailed kisses up to her ear, licking the lobe and then whispering, "I plan to have you so hot you will be begging to come."

"That's not far off already, Master Nico."

"I know ... but you do know your disobedience is call for orgasm denial, don't you?"

"Yes, I know." She wasn't worried. It was actually quite wonderful when he finally allowed her to come. He had denied her before. He was a sensualistic Dom, and he'd make sure all of her senses were aroused before she came, which would make the orgasms that she had with him all the better.

"I see you like the thought of that, my pet."

"I do, Master Nico. I'm finding it hard to think about anything other than what exquisite torture you'll put me through." She'd missed this, missed being close like this with him and letting him take care of her. It was nice not having to worry about anyone else. Not a care in the world but to be his.

Bruno returned with their drinks, setting them down and then just as swiftly leaving.

"Drink up, my sweet, but only enough to get a buzz. I want you cognizant of everything that's happening."

Leaning forward she picked up her glass and settled back against her Master. Nico picked up his drink and raised it up. Felipe and Aurora did the same, so she followed suit.

"To a night of erotic proportions and lust-filled dreams, that each of us will enjoy," Nico announced. They all tapped their glasses together and drank. Then Felipe set his glass down and took Aurora's and put it down as well.

"Come, mi cielo; let's leave these two to their own devices. The Saint Andrew's Cross is waiting for us in our suite." Aurora slipped from his lap and turned back to Nico and Cinda.

"It was a pleasure to meet you, Cinda. I'm sure we'll be seeing a lot of each other. I'm told that you have a real fetish for shoes. I know a great place we can go to sometime, if you wish."

Cinda grinned. "I'm not the only one with that fetish." She nudged Nico and they all laughed. "I'll take you up on that some time." The other couple left, and they settled into a comfortable silence as they drank their drinks. Cinda knew that this was Nico's way of having her anticipate what would happen once they were done. He'd place the occasional kiss to the side of her neck. All the while his hard shaft pressed against her was a telling sign that he was just as horny as she was.

"I can smell how wet you are, Cin. Tonight is all about showing you what you've been missing all these years. What you've kept from the both of us." She took another drink from her glass then set it down. She was starting to feel nice and fuzzy. He'd told her to drink just enough but not to become drunk. She would not disobey him.

"Forgive me, Master Nico, for running."

"Oh you're already been forgiven, though you will still be punished. Do you understand why, Cinda?"

"Yes, it's a matter of me putting my trust in you. Trusting you to take care of me and give me everything I need. By running I placed my trust in myself and not in you."

She truly did understand why she was to be punished. She'd signed a contract with him then run out on it. A good submissive didn't do that. There was still so much hanging in the balance, but she was going to live in the moment and let the rest take care of itself. By the end of this weekend she'd know whether she'd stay or go.

"Good girl. Now we're going to go to the suite. It's time to let me take care of you."

She stood and waited for him to lead the way. When he wrapped his arm about her waist and pulled her close to his side and led her away from the table, it was the safest she'd felt in a long time and the most cherished.
***

Nico gazed over at Cinda as she strolled towards the spot he told her to stand in. It was the suite they'd used five years ago, and it hadn't changed. The walls had mirrors all around, and there was a large canopy bed off to the left side along with nightstands on either side of the bed. He'd also had a table placed in the room that held the items for their play. She hesitated briefly by the table, running her fingertip along the edge. She hesitated at the flogger, and he smiled then cleared his throat. He'd had her pause there and so that he could look over her outfit. He hadn't been able to admire her while they took care of the earlier business. Right now all he wanted to do was take her in and appreciate the woman she'd become in the last five years.

He didn't just want her because she was gorgeous, though that was indeed the case. No, he loved her because of her kindness towards others and her willingness to do whatever she could to please others. No matter what it cost her, Cinda was someone you could depend on. It was time for her to rely on someone else.

That someone else was him, and he'd make sure by the end of this weekend that she admitted that. There was no going back. He couldn't let her go. Now he had to make sure she realized her own worth and that reaching out and taking what she wanted and being cared for wasn't a bad thing. He settled in the chair that had been placed in the middle of the large suite, letting his eyes roam from her stilettos and then slowly up those impossibly long mocha-colored legs in the barely there dress.

Her chest rose quickly under the fabric, her breasts straining against the cloth, allowing him to see that her nipples were hard. He fixed his emerald-colored eyes on her chocolate ones. He brought his fingers up to absently stroke over his goatee as he let her wait before he spoke to her. Anticipation was the key. He wanted her so revved up that she had no choice but to turn to him for what she needed.

"Do you remember our first night together? Why I stopped you and asked you to dance?"

Cinda nodded her head. "I remember, Master Nico." He wiggled his finger for her to come forward and held his hand up when she stood right between his legs. He widened his legs so that there was a bit of space on the chair.

"Put your heel right there." He pointed to the space. Obediently she did so, letting the tip of her shoe slide slowly over his crotch. He smiled. Bringing his hands to her raised calf he stroked his fingers along her skin, caressing softly before he cupped the stiletto in his hand.

"You know I still have the shoe you left back at my office." He held her gaze and watched her nod.

"Yes ... yes," she cleared her throat, "Yes, Master Nico."

"These are gorgeous as well. I'm going to fuck you in them." He watched as she bit her bottom lip.

"Like that, do you? You may not have realized it, but you wore this outfit for me and only for me."

"I love it when you talk to me like that. I'm so wet right now." She gasped as he leaned close and nipped the side of her calf. "Ohhh god, mmm, that feels so good."

"We're talking about the first time I saw you. You were out on the dance floor, dancing with someone else. Your dress was so short I could almost see your ass cheeks peeking out from under it and you had these insanely high heels on. Remember?" He nipped her again and she groaned.

"Mmm ... yes, I remember." He trailed fingers up her leg to her thigh, stroking the skin softly.

"I want you to undress and stand right there in the middle of this room in your heels."

There was a twinkle in her eye when she picked her foot up from the chair and once again brushed it against his hard cock.

"You know, my dear, you're going to pay for that."

"Yes, I know. I'm counting on it." She squealed when he slapped her ass as she turned away from him. He watched her hips sway as she walked away from him and got into position.

"I want you to do it nice and slow," he ordered her softly. He undid his pants, reaching in and taking out his cock. He gripped himself tightly and began to stroke. He watched as her pink tongue ran slowly over her lips, that spark still in her eyes.

Chapter Seven

In being submissive to him she felt powerful. She kept one hand on her hip and brought the other to the zipper that held her dress together, tugging it down slowly and baring every inch of skin until the zipper was just under her full breasts. She left it there, pausing for a few seconds as she dipped her fingers in between her breasts. She thought of the toys that he had on the table; she was in for it with him. Her legs trembled.

"More," Nicolai said.

He was leisurely stroking his cock, from time to time fisting the head of it. She clenched her thighs together in desire when he leaned back in the chair and cupped his balls with his other hand.

Tugging the zipper down some more, she undid the front clasp of her bra, freeing her breasts from the confines of that red silk.

"Play with your nipples and dance for me like you did that night."

She began swaying gently to some unheard music, teasing her nipples to even harder peaks. The power she had to make him want her occupied her mind and body with an intoxicating feeling. He moved his hand on his cock to the same rhythm that she danced. She spun around so that she was facing away from him like she had been that night.

In a moment she was back in time to five years ago, so caught up in the dance it all felt so real. It was almost as if he were pressed against her as he had been then. His face in the crook of her neck and his arms wrapped tight about her body as they swayed together.

"That's it, Cin, take me back to that time. Make me crave you."

She dipped down until she was holding her ankles, thrusting her ass backwards as she did that night. She could almost feel his dick pressed against her ass like it was there. She rose slowly, caressing her own legs as she did so. Turning back as slow as she could with her hand back on her zipper, she undid the dress until it just hung open. Her red thong matched the silk demi-bra.

She shrugged out of the dress, kicking it out of the way. Covering her breasts with one arm, she brushed the straps of her bra off one shoulder, shrugging out of it then doing the same with the other until the bra dropped to the floor. The only thing she was wearing now was her thong and six-inch heels.

"I've changed my mind. Keep the thong on and bring the flogger to me." His voice was husky yet still it held so much authority. Eagerly she went to the table, grabbing the flogger and bringing it to him. He took it from her, though one hand still held his cock. The pre-cum glistened on the thick bulbous head. She licked her lips, aching to taste him.

"Suck me, Cin. It's been too long since I've felt your mouth on me. Though only once, you're due a spanking."

God, she'd missed being spanked by him. Unquestioningly she got to her knees in front of him as he pointed his cock towards her. She licked the head, loving the saltiness and the flavor that was uniquely him. He grabbed her hair and drew her head back, thrusting his cock into her mouth. She moaned around his cock and heard him hiss with pleasure. He thrust into her mouth a few times then stopped to let his cock rest between her lips.

"It's been so long I almost lost it inside your beautiful mouth, Cinda."

He tapped her cheek lightly, her signal to remove her lips from around his cock. She did so, though not without allowing her tongue to lick his prick as he slipped from her lips.

"I didn't want to stop."

"There's time enough for that later. Right now you have a debt to fulfill."

Acceptance trickled through every part of her body. "I know what I need to do to please you, Master."

"Yes, I believe you do." She reached down and placed his cock back into his pants, doing them back up. Then she placed herself across his lap, her ass available to him, and the touch of his hand to her bared ass cheeks made her tingle. She was dangling half on his lap, her hands resting against the plush carpet. She was prepared for her punishment.

"Damn, baby, I love your ass, so beautiful." She whimpered as he kissed one ass cheek and then the other. He hooked his finger and teasingly snapped the strip of fabric at her waist. He laid the flogger on her lower back, and then used his hands to knead the fleshy part of her ass cheeks. Nico eased the straps of her thong down over her hips, and then took it off of her as if it offended him. He returned his attention back to her ass. A few times he'd dip his fingers between her thighs and stroke over her wet pussy lips. It was exquisite torture not knowing just when he'd strike.

"You belong with me." She felt the sting of the flogger as he hit her with it.

She arched into the smack to her ass with a purred moan. The burn from the flogger was exquisite. He smacked both cheeks in tandem, and all she could do was dig her nails into the shag carpet and roll with it.

"Yes, oh god yes, I belong to you." Her ass was on fire, the stinging radiating from her ass to her clit.

"No more running, do you hear me, Cinda?" Each word was emphasized with a smack of the flogger. She knew her ass had to be a bright red. She jerked against him as he smacked her ass again when she didn't say anything.

"I'm sorry, Master Nico. Yes, I hear you, I'm yours."

"Get up, my pet, and go lie down in the middle of the bed on your back. Make sure you put a pillow up under your hips." She lifted herself off of his lap and stepped towards the bed. Cinda situated herself according to his orders, loving how exposed she felt. Her ass still burned from the flogging he'd given her. *God, a spanking had never felt so good.*

From her place on the bed she eyed him as he stood, stripping out of his clothing at a leisurely pace. He laid each piece out over the chair neatly. It was all to show her patience. Her master never rushed anything, most especially their pleasure. The years had been extremely kind to Nico and his body was a powerfully honed machine. He was lean and muscled, strength in every line. Both of his biceps sported intricate Celtic tribal tattoos.

"How's that fine ass of yours?"

"It's still burning, Master Nico."

"It's just as it should be." She saw the small smirk on his beautiful lips. "I think you like me spanking you, making that sweet ass of yours burn."

"You're right, Master Nico. I love it when you reprimand me."

"Hmm, perhaps I need to do something else to make sure you're learning your lesson."

"I'll accept whatever punishment you decide to give me."

"Oh there is no doubt that you will. Time for running is over. You've realized that and now we move forward."

Nico was right. What bothered her was that when the fear of losing control set in and the thought that she needed to keep an orderly life crept in, would she feel the same way? *Breathe. Don't think about it ... breathe.* She let out a slow, cleansing breath. When she opened her eyes again, she noted that Nico was at the table. He set the flogger down and then picked up the rope, lighter and Japanese drip candles.

"You need to learn to let go and let someone else take care of you."

He strode over to the bed, placing the items down as he loomed over her. He looked so powerful and so able to take on any of her monsters. Hell, he and Dr. Fairee had all but gotten rid of her problematic stepsisters. Yes, they were balking at the very idea that they'd have to relinquish hold of the business her father built. She didn't think even they could hold on and do battle with Nico. Only time would tell.

The true issue wasn't the stepsisters. The issue was that she'd run from the only thing in her life that had made her happy. She now had the chance to rectify it, though her modus operandi was always run first, think about it later. But in her heart of hearts she hoped she could stop running away from Nico and run straight into his arms.

"Give me your arms."

She did so eagerly, holding both hands out to him. He didn't say anything else as he tied them with the red-colored rope then secured her arms to the headboard with that rope. Nico then took her feet and secured them to the footboard. She was well and truly trussed up for his inspection, nothing left to the imagination at this point.

She snapped from her reverie when Nico pinched her nipple. That was a surefire way to get her attention. Bringing her gaze up to his, she bit her bottom lip.

"I think a little art work is called for."

"Art work?"

"Mhmm, art work with the candles."

Wax play. One thing she loved more than the burn of the flogger on her ass was the stinging pleasure-pain from the wax as it hit her body and hardened. She moaned softly.

"Please…" It was all she said, but it was enough for him to move into action and grab a candle. It was long, red and tapered. The phallic shape of that candle was enough to keep her as wet as she already was. She was so revved up and so ready for him that she was leaking on the pillow and wetting it.

"You're almost ready for me."

"Almost?" She could not keep the disbelief out of her voice. *How could he say almost?* The way she was feeling in that moment she could come if he just blew air across her clit, which was throbbing.

"Just as I said, almost. You, my pet, will wait to come. You will not orgasm before I say you can. So yes, you're almost ready for me." She heard the emphasis he placed on the word almost. She watched the flickering flame as he lit the candle. Then he tossed the lighter onto the nightstand. It hit with a small sound that carried through the room.

He raised the candle above her and tipped it so that a small stream of wax dripped across her left breast, and she groaned, gripping the ropes that held her tight to the bed. The slight pain that radiated through her body was eclipsed by the pleasure she received from the wax. Soon she was covered in several streams of the wicked wax, her body humming with desire.

"Tell me what you want." He held the candle just over her spread legs, tempting her with the delicious taste of ecstasy that the heated liquid would cause.

"I want that on my clit, Master Nico, please pour it on my clit." Her body tingled with the residual effects of the Japanese wax.

"Since you beg so prettily, my pet, I will give you the very desire of your heart." Nico tipped the candle. The hot wax hit her wet clit and she let out a loud mewl, thrashing against her bindings. She rolled her hips against the pillow, arching her back wanting—no—needing for him to touch her in some way to let her come.

"Please, Master Nico…" She wailed. "I can't wait any longer."

"Who alone will give you your climax, pet? Who will you trust to give you what you need?" he demanded as he blew out the candle and set it on the nightstand. She heard some shuffling and then the crinkle of foil. Turning to look at him she saw him putting on a condom.

"You, I will trust you, Master Nico."

Cinda heard Nico growl and he moved between her legs, one hand gripping her thigh and the other holding his cock. He thrust into her quickly and didn't stop his thrusting as he stared her in the eyes. She tried to close her eyes and opened them immediately when he started to withdraw.

"No!" she uttered.

"Then keep your damn eyes open. I want you to see me. Really see me and know who has your back in all things. You're mine, and I'm tired of you thinking otherwise." He powered into her hard and fast, his curved and thick cock hitting her g-spot with every lunge. It was heaven; she'd missed having him inside of her. No one's cock had ever filled her like Nico's. Every thick, veined inch gave her the sensation of being stuffed. She loved it.

He surged against her, the friction grinding him into her clit. Since she was tied the only thing she could do was go along for the ride and use her inner muscles to hold on as tightly to him as she could. Finally when she could take it no longer she begged him to let her come.

"Master, please!" she keened.

"Since you've been such a good girl ... come for me," he ordered. "Give me your cream, my pet."

She needed no further urging. She came hard and fast on his cock, and she was so wet that he almost slipped from her more than once. He dug his hands into her hips, keeping her in place, and then he too was wracked with convulsions, crashing into her and groaning out her name.

He pushed his face into the side of her neck, placing small kisses on her neck and then on her chest. The heat of his lips made her shiver, her body still wracked with the pleasurable contractions caused by the hard orgasm.

He laid his body on top of hers, as both of them fought to catch their breath. She wanted to hold him, yet she could not. Not until he freed her from her bindings. To be denied something so simple was a pleasure in itself. It made it all the more wonderful when she could give in to the desire. Her master was attuned to what she needed, and tonight had been no different.

***

"Tell me that what we have doesn't matter, Cinda." His breath was hot against her throat, which was damp with her perspiration. She moaned when he licked the small indention at her throat.

"I can't."

"Right, you can't because it would be a lie."

"You're right, Master Nico. If I said that, it would be a lie."

"It's about time you admitted as much."

When she didn't say anything he nipped her neck and arched away, though he made sure to keep himself within her. The wax was flaking and warming between them, and he'd have to get up soon to clean her but not yet.

He had to look in her eyes and see for himself that what she was saying was what she wanted. Nicolai saw her eyes shimmering with tears. He watched as her mouth opened, closed and then reopened. When she still didn't speak he cupped her cheek in his palm, stroking his thumb along her cheek.

"I'm not letting you go this time. I don't care if your sisters fight this tooth and nail. You're where you belong, with me. End of story."

"End of story?"

He nodded his head. "Yes, end of story for them. They are a closed chapter in your life now. If I have to pay them off, I will, but no longer will your life be spent serving them. Especially seeing as they don't have your full interest at heart. No longer will they use you. Your place is at my side as my girl."

"My place is truly at your side. You're right, and I've been foolish. I want to enjoy this time with you. Please, no more talk of them until we have to."

"I'm in full agreement with that."

He groaned as he slipped out of her, settling on his knees between her legs. After one last look at Cinda, he got out of the bed and disposed of the condom in the small trashcan next to the bed, then left for the bathroom. He cleaned himself quickly and returned with a wet, warm cloth and cleaned her gently. He could tell she was tired, and he wasted no time in undoing her bindings so that she could relax. Once he was done cleaning her and had put the cloth away, he stood next to the bed.

"Under the covers with you, Cin, I can see you're tired. We will rest for a while, and then I have to have you again."

She complied, and he got in, pulling her close to his side. She laid her head on his chest and tucked her head under his chin.

"You're right. This is how it should be."

Kissing the top of her head, he heard and felt her breath become even, letting him know she would soon be asleep. Nothing more need be said. He had what he wanted, and he sure as hell had to ensure she got what she wanted.

Chapter Eight

The weekend had passed in a lust-filled blur for Cinda, and she hadn't wanted it to end. She sat up in the bed, holding the sheet to her chest as if it would stop the day from ending. When she'd awaken she'd found that Nico had already left the bed, though his side was still warm. Her body ached in places she hadn't known existed.

The suite door opened and Nico, fully dressed with the exception of shoes, stepped in holding a tray with that held a silver coffee pot and she was sure other things she couldn't see.

"You're awake, my sweet, good to see. Ready for breakfast, Cinda?"

"Yes, Master Nico. I find that I'm starving." She grinned.

"I know what that twinkle in your eyes means. Though I'm hungry for more than food right now just like you are, you need to eat." He set the tray in front of her and she looked down to see a perfectly cooked steak, eggs, toast, juice and a cup of coffee.

"Mmm, it smells perfect. Are you going to eat with me?"

"I ate already. I'll sit here with you while you eat. We gave to meet up with Doctor Fairee in about an hour. So you have time to eat and shower." He kissed her forehead then settled down next to her on his side of the bed.

"It's a shame you're dressed already," she teased, picking up the fork and cutting up the steak so she could eat it with ease.

"Depending on how fast you get done, we may have a bit of time for a little something."

"A little something, something?"

"Yeah, my girl, a little something, something."

"Does the Doc have anything of importance to tell us?" She could hear the hope in her own voice so she was sure he could hear it as well.

"He hasn't said. I didn't ask as I wanted us to both be there when we heard the news one way or the other." He took the fork from her and forked some of the food and held it up to her lips. "Eat. No time to worry about what's going to happen. We will handle that when the time comes."

She opened her mouth and accepted the food he was feeding her. She'd try to listen to what her master said, but it wasn't easy trying not to worry about what was going on and what may or may not happen. He was right though. She needed to wait to see what Drusilla and Anastasia would do before she even got close to worrying. Nico talked to her through the meal and before she realized it she was done with her breakfast.

With his urging she was finished quicker than she would've been had she allowed herself to dwell on the issue and not have him there to talk with her as she ate. He had a way of making everything better. Nico got up and took her tray, standing next to the bed.

"Go and shower, the clothing I got for you will be laid out when you come out."

"I thought you promised me a little something?"

"Do as I say and who knows." Nico turned and walked away from her, heading towards the door. "Hurry," he said over his shoulder.

Cinda jumped up from the bed and headed towards the bathroom. A shower was in order, a very fast shower at that. She wanted what he promised and nothing was going to stop her from getting it, not even herself.

***

Nico had heard from Doctor Fairee earlier that morning while Cinda slept. The Doctor had warned that the sisters wanted to meet with Cinda before they signed anything. So Nico had told Fairee that he and Cinda would be ready later that morning and ready to speak with the sisters. Felipe had offered his office again for the meeting so that's where it would be happening.

Fairee had a way with making dreams come true. That old man was magic. There was no doubt in Nico's mind that he'd found a way to make things work out for Cinda as well. Walking back into the room after taking the tray to the kitchen, he settled in the large chair next to the bed, waiting for Cinda to finish in the shower. As per his orders the clothing he'd bought for her was laid out on the bed. Set out for her was a beautiful black A-line skirt, a red pair of high heels, garters, bra and a pretty red blouse.

He turned towards the sound of the bathroom door opening and smiled as she stepped out, still wet from the shower. She walked towards him, her hips swaying, and he couldn't take his eyes off of her. She paused right in front of his chair, a wicked grin on her lips.

"Permission to sit in your lap, Master Nico?"

"You may sit in my lap facing away from me."

He saw the arch of her brow, but she didn't question him as she rotated away from him, placing her body in his lap. He pulled her snuggly to himself and kissed her wet shoulder. He didn't care that she was wetting his clothing. She'd pulled her hair up into a ponytail for her shower so her neck and shoulders were fair game for his mouth. He took in the scent that was uniquely her and growled softly. He felt her shiver.

He set his hands on her thighs, squeezing gently, and he heard the catch in her breath. Nipping her neck for a few heated seconds until she began moving restlessly in his lap he chuckled softly. He slowly slid one hand up her stomach to her breast, cupping it and putting his lips to her ear.

"What do you want, my girl?"

"Your touch everywhere." Her voice was raspy.

"My touch, or will anyone's touch do?" He flicked his tongue against her earlobe and pinched her nipple between his fingers as he waited for her answer.

"Yours and only yours. That is, unless it is your wish for me to have another's touch."

"Good answer, pet. As your master I know what you need. Have you finally come to full realization of that?"

"Yes … oh yes. You have my best interests at heart." He tugged at her nipple, and she whimpered.

"So when we get into this meeting with your sisters, no matter the outcome, who will you leave with?" He brushed his fingers over the lips of her pussy. She was as wet as ever.

"Ohhh god!"

"Not the answer I was looking for," he teased her.

Her laugh was a bit drawn out as she rocked her hips, trying to rub herself into his fingers, which he kept away from her clit on purpose.

"You, Master Nico. I'll be leaving with you!" The last word was a scream as he pressed his fingers to her clit and began to rub furiously. She arched back against him, rocking into his hand and moaning his name.

He slowly circled her entrance with two fingers then thrust them in deeply to the hilt, loving the wet, silken sensation being inside of her in any form conjured in his mind. Pressed for time, he fucked her hard and fast. Cinda locked her legs around his wrist as she rode him, keeping him deep within. She cried out his name, sobbing as she came in a heated rush on his fingers, her nails digging into his pants leg as she jerked in the throes of passion until she was well and truly spent and lying against him shuddering.

Nico waited until Cinda's breathing evened out. "Now we will both go to the meeting smelling like the other. No one will mistake that you're mine, no one." Taking his fingers from her, he licked them clean then stood, carrying her to the bed and then placing her on her feet.

"Dress, Cinda, we're going to go and meet up with Doc and your sisters."

***

Cinda and Nico sat at the large office table with her sisters on the other side and Doctor Fairee at the head of the table. Both sisters were dressed dramatically in all black. They even had ugly hats perched on their heads. It reminded Cinda of a scene in the movie where a husband and wife were getting a divorce. What were the words that described a divorce? Irreconcilable differences?

From the look on Dru's and Ana's faces, that was what this was going to come down to. She'd spoken briefly with Doctor Fairee, and it was obvious her sisters were still trying to hold out. Now it was time to get to the nitty-gritty of it all. She faced her sisters with dignity, waiting for Fairee to speak, but no such thing happened when one of the women could not control herself.

"It's unfair what you're doing to us, Cinda!" Anastasia blurted out.

Drusilla cast Ana an ugly scowl then turned her ire on Cinda.

"It's extremely unfair for you to think that we should have to live on a stipend when we have been getting more than that since Mom died."

Cinda was about to speak when Nico's hand suddenly gripped her leg and he squeezed. She sat back in the chair and waited.

"Is it fair that the two of you have ridden on the coattails of not only Cinda's father but also of Cinda?"

Drusilla huffed and her glare deepened, but she didn't say anything.

"Nothing to say to that, Drusilla?" Nico questioned.

"We deserve more than you're offering us!" Drusilla, it seemed, refused to look at Nico or address him. That pissed Cinda off. She grabbed Nico's hand and squeezed. He leaned in and whispered in her ear.

"Go ahead, my sweet. It's time they know that you can't be walked on."

"What you're being offered is better than what you'd get if you continue to fight this," Cinda stated. "My father worked hard for the business. It's not a Fortune 500 business, but it is his legacy. My legacy from my father that I plan to keep, and you two will no longer rule me."

Doctor Fairee stood and strolled calmly around the table to stand. He placed a silver pen and papers in front of Drusilla and Anastasia.

"Now, dear ladies, we are back to square one. Our visit the other day with the examiner proved that there was indeed a forgery. So your only option available is to either accept the generous deal or to go away with nothing."

Anastasia broke the thick silence, her caramel-colored skin mottled with pink. "Cinda, we will accept the deal."

Drusilla gasped and pushed her sister. "What?"

"Dru, you heard exactly what I said. If we don't accept, think of the alternative." Cinda thought it was the most sensible thing that Anastasia had ever said.

Drusilla looked as if she was about to start arguing and Anastasia raised her hand. "No, Dru, this has to stop and if we go any further we won't win. Can't you see that? After all the shit we've put Cinda through she's willing to still take care of us." Anastasia looked Cinda dead in the eyes and for once her sister didn't seem so evil to her.

"We will accept the deal. No more problems from us, I promise."

Drusilla just sat there, stone faced and basically sulking. Before Cinda's very eyes Anastasia had finally come into her own.

"So you agree to have the shares revert back to Cinda, along with actually working at the business and getting a stipend? You both will also be leaving the home and finding your own place. Right?" Doc Fairee said, with his arms crossed over his chest, a small smile on his face.

"Yes, I agree to it all." Anastasia said softly, "Dru?"

"I agree to everything as well." The words were growled out, but it didn't matter to Cinda. She was free. Everything blended together as papers were signed and then her sisters left. Doctor Fairee left soon after, but not without Cinda hugging and kissing him profusely as well as calling him a miracle worker.

***

"For five years I've been lost without you. Yes, there are plenty of other women in this world, but none compare to you. I need you to hear this to know how deeply you're leaving affected me."

Her eyes filled with tears. They were tears of pain, remorse and yes, happiness. One escaped, and he wiped her cheek gently. They were naked and lying on the bed with her on her back and him above her leaning on his elbow and staring down at her.

"Don't tell me your speechless, Cin?"

"I just can't believe I ran and wasted so much—" Nico placed his finger on her lip.

"Stop, I won't allow you to dwell on the past. Yes, we've been apart and it hurt us both. We're together now, and that's all that matters. Our new beginning begins in this moment."

"I want to say something that I didn't say before I ran. When we had the argument at your office when you said I was trying to take the world on my shoulders. I know it's the past, but I want to clear the air. May I, Master Nico?"

"Nothing you say will change my mind about keeping you in my life. Go ahead, Cinda, if telling this makes you feel at peace."

She took his hand and kissed his palm then set it on her cheek so that he was cupping her face.

"I loved you from the moment I met you. That emotion scared the hell out of me and made me think you were too good to be true. Too many people have left my life when I loved them. My mother first and then my father, I didn't want the same thing to happen with you. So I ran. Your words hit too close to home. I was so used to taking care of everyone."

She took a deep breath. "That when you wanted to take care of me I thought it some fluke and that soon you'd tire of me and leave anyway. So I left—"

Nico interrupted her. "You left before I could do the leaving."

She nodded her head. "Yes, that way I wouldn't be hurt. I love you. I'm sorry I didn't trust that you cared for me and truly wanted to take care of me."

"I more than just care for you, Cinda A. Rella. I love you every bit as much as you love me. I want to be the one who gives you your happy ending. All you have to do is let me. Will you?"

The tears fell freely now and she sobbed, nodding her head. "Yes! A million times yes."

"Then we have a wedding to plan."

"Wedding?"

"You didn't think I was just talking about being fuck buddies, did you? I mean that's all well and good and we definitely are going to do loads of fucking. That's not all I'm offering. I want to marry you. Will you marry me, Cinda? Take my ring and my collar?"

"Yes, I will take your ring and collar, Master Nico, and hold them near and dear to my heart."

He kissed her soundly, and she wrapped her arms about his neck, kissing him hungrily. Whoever thought there was no such thing as a happy ever after hadn't ever met one such as the good Doctor. Life had a way of coming together when the magic known as Doctor Fairee became involved. She had much to be thankful for and a wedding to plan.

NIKKI PRINCE

RIDIN' RED

DEDICATION

To my girls who help me when I'm stuck on an idea: Piper, Kim, Michelle and Shyla. Thank you so very much for your friendship. Love you bunches. To my readers, thank you for keeping my dream alive.

NIKKI PRINCE

RIDIN' RED

Once Upon a Dream, 3

Nikki Prince

Copyright © 2013

Chapter One

Anastasia Trumane couldn't believe her misfortune at seeing her old boyfriend and Dom Lucien Wolf at Club Fantasy, where it was said that your fondest wishes come true. *Shit, did I wish him up?* She frowned as she stood in the hotel room she had been renting with her sister since Cinda had evicted them a few weeks ago. What a long story that was. Actually, it was more of a nightmare than anything else, a nightmare that she and Drusilla had caused.

It remained a rainy, dreary day, and the rain pelted the window. She couldn't get rid of the feeling that what was happening was just another sign that things could swiftly go from bad to worse. It wasn't that she was upset with Cinda, because she and Drusilla deserved everything that had happened to them. It wasn't Cinda's fault that karma had finally caught up with them and now was kicking them in the ass.

Why had she listened to Drusilla? She'd gone to the club, following Drusilla like a little puppy. How could she have known that Lucien would be there? That he'd still look so damn good she wanted to lick every last ab and finish that off with riding him until she was screaming his name? She pressed her forehead against the window pane and closed her eyes.

"Lucien, please. I don't want to go." She could hear the urgency in her own voice.

"You have to go. I neither want nor need you in my life."

"What the hell could have changed from last night to make you say that?"

He looked so impassive standing there with his arms across his chest and actually barring her from entering his condo.

"Take your things and go, Ana. I don't want to see you again. I will no longer be your Dom, and you are no longer tied to me as my submissive." And with those words he turned his back on her and went into his place, closing the door in her face. He'd left her on his doorstep with her suitcases and her dreams turning to shit.

"Ana!" Drusilla's screeching pulled her from her daydreaming, and she turned to look at her sister who was sitting on one of the double beds painting her toenails. Dru had the craziest expression.

"Yes, Dru?"

"I've been talking to you for the past ten minutes. What the hell are you thinking about that you're not paying attention to me?"

"Sorry, I sorta zoned out." She'd been trying to ignore her sister's incessant chatting.

"Yeah, I can tell. I said your name five times. Now where was I? What did you want to do tonight?"

"I hadn't thought that far."

"Well, I'm tired of being cooped up in here and not going anywhere. So if you want to go with me then get ready. If not, I'm heading out. Perhaps go to a club tonight."

She didn't want to go to a club. She wanted to stay in the room, and yes, mope. Okay, well, maybe not mope, but she wanted to remember the last time she'd been really happy and try to figure out a plan to get that way again.

"You go ahead, Dru. I'm not feeling well. I'll stay here." Her sister rolled her eyes and made a huffing sound then shrugged.

"Suit yourself. You need to get laid."

Leave it to Dru to make it sound so visceral. So blunt and mannish.

"You're probably right about that, but yeah, I'm fine." She turned back towards the window and saw that the rain was lifting. It was a perfect time to order in and get cozy in the bed with a good book. If she couldn't have her Prince Charming like Cinda, perhaps she could dream about having one and live vicariously through fiction. Love was a fantasy anyway. If she'd learned anything from her encounter with Luc, it was that love was fleeting and not real.

Drusilla sniggered from her corner of the room, but Anastasia didn't bother to look around. "Fine? Fine, you say? Hmmph, not even close, but if you like it, I love it."

Drusilla didn't say anything more and for that Anastasia was thankful. At this point in her life, she was getting tired of Dru's incessant opinions and whining. It was getting harder and harder to ignore her. So it was best Dru was going out for the night.

She was a fool. All this time and she was still wondering what Lucien was up to. He'd kicked her to the curb, not the other way around, so she supposed that was the reason she still thought of him. She wanted to touch him, to kiss him, to melt into his touch and be called his baby girl once more. Those were all foolish dreams. The derision on his face when he'd seen her at the club had been potent.

The guards had separated her from Drusilla in the beginning and as luck would have it, Lucien was given the task of watching her until he'd been relieved of his post. He'd stood at the door not talking to her; it was the worst thing of all to have his silence.

"Lucien," she'd said softly. He hadn't even turned her way. He just stared straight ahead.

"Please, Luc, talk to me." That was when he'd turned to look at her.

"What is it you want me to say, Ana?" Eyes as blue as ice bore into her, making her shiver and want to hide herself from his gaze.

"I don't know, but I don't want you to just stand there as if we don't know one another."

"The Ana I knew before wouldn't have done what happened here tonight."

"You're probably right about that. Though the Ana you knew is no longer. You made sure of that when you made me leave." Luc had frowned, his lips tightening, and just when she thought he'd say something in his defense, the door had opened.

Those last words had ended their conversation as he'd once again turned into 'Captain-don't-give-a-fuck.' The owner of the club had come in, and there wasn't a chance to even come close to talking to him again.

The one thing that remained a constant was the need she was feeling for a man who wanted nothing to do with her. Absently, she listened to Drusilla moving about the room and getting ready for her night on the town. The single nice thing was that Dru would party until it was the next day and at least she wouldn't have to be bothered with her fussing or trying to steer her in any one direction. She didn't know how long she stood there looking out the window. The silence was beautiful, only to be cut by the sound of Drusilla leaving, and she wasn't even sure if she'd said goodbye.

Maybe a nice warm shower would cool the ardor rushing through her body. She'd do anything to forget him, to stop the dreams that only held his image and his touch. Turning she strolled to the bathroom, stripping out of her shorts and tank top, tossing them into the small hamper in the bathroom. She gathered her hair into a bun and pinned it up.

She adjusted the water to the heated temperature she liked and stepped in, closing the sliding glass door and letting the water hit her body full blast. Bracing herself with her hands she leaned forward, placing her face into the water. Anastasia grabbed her cloth that was hanging in the shower and lathered it after leaning back. Her body still hummed with unrequited desire. *Fuck, it was going to be a long, long night.*

Perhaps Drusilla was right, She needed to get good and nailed by some unnamed, faceless cock. She didn't want to know who fucked her. She wanted hard and fast sex. The man or men who gave that to her didn't have to be someone she knew; in fact, she preferred it if she didn't know them. Anonymous sex. It was fast becoming a craving. Hard, quick, and animalistic.

She cupped her wet breasts, which were heavy and achy and in dire need of being sucked and licked.

Slowly she pulled and tugged at both nipples, a moan tumbling forth from her parted lips. Her hands were no substitute for the rough and callused hands of a man. They'd have to do. She rested back against the cool shower tile, one hand cupping her breast and the other moving down slowly to cup her pussy and tease over her clit. Her labia was swollen, and she was wet.

Fire speared through her, and the only way to assuage the need was to plunge two fingers knuckles deep into her aching, weeping pussy and fuck herself. It wasn't going to take long for her to come at all. Her inner muscles were already clamping down on her fingers and drawing them in deep. Soon she was dreaming it was Luc touching her and bringing her to the edge. That imagery pulled her straight into a much needed orgasm, and she came hard, screaming his name as it echoed through the small room.

It wasn't enough, yet it had to be. There was no more Luc and Ana. Not wanting to dredge up any other old memories of him, she quickly showered then got out, and pulling on a fluffy hotel robe, she exited the bathroom. The nice thing that Cinda had done for them was make it possible that they could still live in some ease. She owed her some thanks, for truly she hadn't had to do even that. She dressed and then pulled back the covers, grabbed her book and was about to settle into the bed to read when there was a knock at the door.

Chapter Two

Who on earth could that possibly be?

"Just a second," she called out.

What if something had happened to Dru? As much as Dru pissed her off, she didn't want anything to happen to her. She hurried to the door, unlocked it and jerked it open. Her eyes widened, and she stood there with her mouth agape.

"Hello, Red."

Still she couldn't find her speech. Her fantasy come to life stood in the doorway. The pet name he'd given her flowed like honey off his tongue.

"Going to let me in?"

"No!" She proceeded to shut the door, and he stopped it with his booted foot.

"Come now, Red, let me in…"

"Leave, Luc. We have nothing to say to one another that hasn't already been said."

"Is that any way to treat an old friend?"

"Friends? Is that what we are?" *Why does he have to look and smell so good? Why is he here?*

"We were more than friends once, Red."

"I seem to recall you're the reason that ended. Now please, just go." He didn't budge, and she let out a sound of frustration. They'd be at this all night; he was as stubborn as hell. She held the door open. "Come in and say what you want, then go."

"Thank you, Red."

"Don't thank me just yet. I may just fucking kick you in the balls as retribution." He entered the suite, and she closed the door, turning to watch him warily.

"I'd more than deserve that."

"Get to talking, Lucien."

"Since our encounter at the club, you haven't been far from my mind."

She gave a small sniff. "The fuck you say."

He held up his hand. "Please let me finish."

She sighed and crossed her arms over her chest, focusing her eyes on the lamp just behind his shoulder. Never him. If she looked at him, all would be lost. Just being this close to him had her heart racing. It was so loud she marveled that he couldn't hear it.

"Finish, please. I was just about to read and turn in for the night." Damn, she sounded so exciting.

"The Ana I knew didn't turn in early."

"You never really knew me, Lucien."

"Fair enough. I want to remedy that. Let me get to know you."

She brought her eyes to his quickly. "You've got to be fucking kidding me, Lucien Wolf." That was when she noticed he'd taken advantage of her not looking at him and was now only inches from her. She stepped back until she was forced against the door.

"You smell so good, Red." He wasn't touching her yet, his hands on either side of her head on the door. His lips inches from hers, his warmth emitting from him, the unique scent that was his wafted about, and she groaned. He put his nose to the pulse at her throat, and she whimpered.

"Stop…" It sounded weak even to her ears.

"You just came, Red. I can smell it on you. Fuck, too bad I wasn't here."

Those words galvanized her into action, and she pushed against his chest. Of course, he was resistant and didn't budge. The heat of his skin through his black t-shirt seared her. She drew her hands away and fast.

He grabbed one of her hands and placed it back on his chest over his heart and held it there all the while his ice-colored gaze held hers. He made her feel so small in comparison. At 6'6" he dwarfed her.

"I don't have time for games, Lucien. Stop this. Whatever this is, you need to stop it."

"Feel my heart, Ana, my sweet." His heart beat strongly beneath her fingers, the cadence mesmerizing.

"Luc—" he cut her off.

"No, listen. It was a mistake to make you leave. I tried to stay away, but seeing you a few weeks ago just brought to light that I shouldn't have ever let you go."

"How did you find me?"

"Cinda told me where you were. I asked her, though it took a bit of cajoling. She didn't understand how I even knew you."

"I kept my time with you my secret. I didn't share it with anyone, least of all Cinda. She and I, if you haven't noticed, aren't close. Though that little problem is mostly by my design and Drusilla's," she half-muttered to herself.

"Listen, Red, I know I don't deserve to ask you this, but I want another chance."

"I'm not the same person, Lucien. You said it yourself. There is no going back."

"I'm not asking to go back, baby girl. I'm asking to go forward." He cupped her cheek, and then stroked his fingertip along her earlobe. She shivered. It was his signature move with her and in the next moment his hands were at her throat. He used his thumbs to stroke up and down both sides of her neck as he held her. She bit her lip in reaction. The years slipped away, and she was a submissive to his master again. There was a time when she'd have done anything he asked. Had that changed? It was a question she didn't know the answer to, least not yet. Part of her wanted to tell him to leave, to never come back. The other part of her wanted to hold on tight to him and never let him go.

"Luc, some things we are never meant to go back to." All the while what ran through her head was not looking him in the eyes. There was something about his gaze that seemed to capture her soul.

"Look at me, baby." Fuck, a command. An order that she was hard pressed to refuse. He had to know she was in his thrall when she did it. Perhaps this time it wouldn't happen. It had been long enough that his spell couldn't be woven again.

Raising her gaze to his, she was lost. "See me, Red, really see me." Feral, animalistic, all the things she'd craved for so long. She blinked as the image of a large, black wolf loomed before. She gasped and struggled to get out of his grasp. No surprise that she couldn't, but that didn't stop her from crying out and struggling against him.

"Ana, stop! I won't hurt you." He shook her by her arms. She grabbed him by his forearms.

"Let me go! Oh my god, just let me go!" She was shivering, her whole body shaking with fear and emotion.

"Red, please ... if you've never listened to me, do it now. I won't hurt you. I know this is a fucking sucky way to reveal who I am to you. I should have done it years ago."

"You're fucking right you should've! You're a fucking werewolf! How is that even fucking possible?"

"Yes, I'm a werewolf. There are many creatures of legend walking about and hidden from humans. Anastasia, I won't hurt you." Something in his voice calmed her, and she believed him.

"Why?" One word, but it held her heart in it.

"You're my mate."

"Mate, Lucien?" Most would have thought it an odd choice of words. She didn't. She'd always sensed that Lucien was different somehow. There were other beings out there, other than humans. Her sister Drusilla always told her she was silly to fill her head with such nonsense from books.

"Yes, my mate, you're my mate," he repeated yet again.

"Tell me, do you often shun your mates?" She couldn't resist that jab at him. He'd hurt her, and she was going to let him know it. Letting him get away with that would never do.

He winced. "I was young, stupid, and very scared of the responsibilities that were laid at my feet."

"You, afraid?" She frowned. "Impossible."

He chuckled. "I assure you, Red, I've been afraid."

"I can't accept this, Lucien. I have a lot of stuff going on."

"Do you mean your continuing to be under your sister's thumb?"

"What I do is no longer a concern of yours. I'm sure you'll be able to find another mate." Her words were meant to hurt him. They had the desired effect as she watched him grimace, and he took his hands from her body and stood back.

"I know this is a lot to throw at you, all at once."

"You think?" She pushed away from the door and opened it. "You need to go, Lucien. There is nothing for you here." She wrapped her arms around herself, bereft, cold, and definitely at a loss.

For a moment it looked as if he would defy what she asked and then he growled and yanked the door open. "Anastasia, if you change your mind you know where to find me. I'll be at the club. I've already spoken with Doc Fairee, so you'd be allowed there again as my guest."

"You'll be waiting forever, Luc. I won't step foot in that place again."

To Lucien's credit, he didn't say anything more; he closed the door behind him and left.

Chapter Three

Lucien left Anastasia's hotel room and entered the dark hotel parking structure more determined than ever to make her his and Bruno's mate. When he'd told her to leave and never come back it had been because he thought he was saving her. He wasn't human, and he wasn't quite animal. To live between both realms of existence had been hard for him. He hadn't come to terms with it, and telling her to go was what he'd thought best.

He'd been very inaccurate in his thinking. The laws and physics of his attraction to her hadn't just been lust. It had been so much more, a melding of souls. In having sex with her before, he'd bound her to him, starting the ritual of mating that must be completed. Having had sex with her, his DNA and hers had bonded, sealing their fate. She was his more than she'd ever realize. He'd been looking for ways to stop the process all this time.

It was the one thing he'd hope to be able to give her. There was no way scientifically possible to stop their bonding. It was irrevocable, just as his bond was with Bruno. Their need for a mate to consummate into their relationship was fast approaching. The pain that all three would go through the closer they got to that date was going to be hard to cover up, if they didn't spend that time together.

He got into his black SUV and leaned his head back on the car seat, closing his eyes. When the sound of a throat clearing broke through his silence, he didn't open his eyes.

"Did you talk to her? Is she willing?" Bruno Hunter questioned in hushed tones as if there were someone in the darkened structure that could hear them.

It would be actually quite funny if the situation wasn't so serious.

"Yes, I saw her, and no, she isn't willing." He rubbed his hand over his face. He needed to think.

"We need her."

"Yes, we need her Bruno." Even to himself he sounded gruff. Turning his head, he gave Bruno his full attention.

"I more than anyone realize how much we need her, Bruno. I set this in motion, and I will make it right. I promise." He wasn't sure how he could promise anything, but he did it just the same. As much as Ana held his heart, so did Bruno. He'd do anything for the both of them.

The first time he'd met Bruno it had been at the club when he'd hired on to be the bartender. Lucien had a hard and fast rule of not dating anyone he worked with. Playing with them? That was another story. His dealing with Bruno had started as a tryst. He hadn't wanted to get close to anyone after Ana. Before he knew it, Bruno had snuck into his bed and then his heart. The sex between them was explosive, as they were both alpha males and that streak couldn't be tamped down.

"You're tense, Luc. Let me release some of that tension for you."

Lucien knew full well what that meant. He'd give him a blowjob, one that was quick and fast, meant to satisfy him in this moment and get him through to the next. Bruno brought his hands down and undid the zipper of Lucien's jeans. He freed Lucien's thick cock from the confines of those pants and groaned.

"Bruno, you don't have to do this."

"Oh believe me, I know I don't have to do it. I want to though. It's been hours since I had your cock in my mouth. You're all wound up. What kind of mate would I be not to fix that if I can?" Bruno used his free hand to cup Lucien's balls then dipped his head to lick his tongue over the weeping tip.

"Mm, nothing like car sex to release some testosterone."

"This is for you. Relax and enjoy this." When Bruno gave another long swipe of his tongue over the head of his cock, Lucien hissed in pleasure. This wasn't just sex; this was pure unadulterated need.

Unable to resist, he gripped the back of the other man's head, forcing him to take more of his cock into his mouth. Bruno could take a lot. Luc had been with him long enough to know what his limits were along with his fetishes. Bruno prized himself as a connoisseur of cock and damn if he didn't prove it each time.

The long swipe of Bruno's tongue along his shaft and the tightening grip was a sure way to get him to come hard and fast. The alpha rose in him, and he started fucking Bruno's mouth, he pushed more and more of his cock into that willing mouth until he was hitting the back of Bruno's throat. Like a champ, Bruno took all of him and gave all of himself.

"Fuck!" He came hard, his cum spurting into Bruno's mouth, and the man took it in stride, sucking harder and drinking down every last bit of cream that flowed until he'd sucked Lucien dry. Lucien sagged back against the seat, swallowing hard to try to get his breathing back under control. All the while Bruno readjusted Lucien's pants and moved back into his seat as if nothing had happened. *Fuck, he loved him.*

"Better?" Bruno questioned.

"Much better, thank you, B."

"I'd say 'my pleasure', but that went both ways."

"That it did."

"Now I'm sure you're a bit more focused."

"Unquestionably."

Lucien reached over and stroked Bruno's cheek. Looking into eyes as blue as his own, he could feel the wolf just beneath the surface calling to his. Bruno was of biracial descent, a striking male with olive-toned skin and a body that was rock hard and drool-worthy. Anyone would want him, but Lucien had been blessed to have him.

"She doesn't know about me, does she?"

"No, it would have been too much to drop on her at once. She just now found out my true nature. She was afraid, but we were together a long while and I did her no harm. I think that's what softened the blow."

Bruno nodded his head.

"From what I've seen of her, we have our work cut out for us. She was quite a spitfire at the club a few weeks ago."

"True, but most of that has to do with being led around by her sister Drusilla and my ill treatment of her. I should've kept her with me."

"Luc, looking back like that isn't going to change anything. When we get her back, you can apologize then."

"I don't know what I'd do without you, B. I love you."

"I feel the same about you, and let's hope you never have to think about doing without me."

Luc dipped his head in agreement, righted himself in the seat, and then started the car. He had to speak with Doc Fairee. It was time to get the man of magic in on this. Everything Doctor Fairee touched turned to gold; he wanted the same to happen with his, Ana's and Bruno's lives.

"Where we headed?" Bruno said.

"Going to go and see Fairee. If anyone can help it would be him, right along with Felipe. The club isn't just for everyone else; we can find our wishes too. I found you there … didn't I?" They both chuckled.

"True, you did hit the mother lode when you found me." Bruno's tone was teasing.

"That I did, that I did."

"I can smell her on you. If it were anyone else, I'd be pissed."

"You're not pissed off because she's our other part. Through her scent you can smell the connection."

"How long do we have, Luc?"

"We have until her birthday to claim her as our own." He didn't divulge how much time that gave them. Bruno was a smart man and picked up on that point.

"Which is when, Lucien?"

"We have until the end of the month, which is a week from now and then it's her birthday. We have to claim her before or on that day."

"To Fairee's it is."

He recognized no matter what Bruno had his back and in this, their cause, it wasn't any different.

"If anyone can help us, it would be him."

"I don't disagree at all, Luc. I'm with you on this."

Lucien's cell rang. He pushed a button on the car's stereo so he could take the call through Bluetooth. He tapped on the speaker, as he had nothing to hide from Bruno.

"Lucien."

"Lucien, my boy, glad I got ahold of you." The voice of Doctor Godwin Fairee filled the vehicle.

"Damn, Doc, you must be psychic. I was just heading your way."

"Oh yes, I had a feeling that you needed me. Is it time to bring your fantasy into the light?"

He glanced at Bruno, and Bruno shrugged his shoulders. There was a look of disbelief on this face as well. He put his eyes back on the road.

"Bruno and I need you to work your magic. Anastasia is resistant to regular persuasion. You'd offered the use of the club, and we wish to take that avenue. I know I said I wanted to try to go the normal route. Well, the situation is anything but normal."

"I've already spoken with Felipe. The club is yours to use. As it is with everyone, just fill out the proper paperwork and everything will be nice and tidy."

"We have a matter of needing to have everything done within a certain time frame."

"I remember. Say nothing more. Your wish is my command." The old man chuckled, and then the phone went dead.

"If anyone can do it … Fairee can," Bruno said in a reassuring voice.

"Exactly."

"How do you think he'll do it, Luc?"

"I don't know. It's like you said, though, if anyone can do it, Fairee can." There was no need to head to Fairee's now, so he whipped the car back around and headed for home. He needed a run and was quite certain that Bruno could do with one too. He wouldn't worry about how or why she got there. He knew it would be done. The old man discerned wishes and had enough balls to see them through.

Chapter Four

Her feet and back ached. Manual labor was definitely something she hadn't been used to. She was actually starting to like it. Her sister Dru thought she was crazy, wondering how she could even possibly like such demeaning work as vacuuming, dusting, and cleaning toilets.

She'd of course told Drusilla that it was an honest pastime and she was now truly being a productive member of society. *There was nothing like working for a living to make you appreciate everything you had.* Why it took her this long she didn't know, but she needed to speak with Cinda and to thank her.

She looked up from wiping down some desks that were in the office she was currently cleaning and gasped. A large black man with the prettiest eyes she'd ever seen stood in the doorway.

"Sorry, little lady, I didn't mean to startle you."

Damn, his voice was deep and sexy too. The baritone sent shivers along her spine. She hadn't thought anyone could make her instantly wet but Lucien. She was wrong, very wrong.

"How did you get in here? No one else is supposed to be in here." Her voice was accusatory, and she stood, crossing her arms over her chest.

"You didn't lock the door."

"Oh." How stupid of her.

"I'm not going to hurt you. I have a message to give you."

"A message?"

"Yes, Cinda and Nico wanted you to know that you need to come to the club in order to get your stipend. There was a problem with the bank transfers. They're not sure what it is. I was sent to give you that info."

"Okay … why couldn't she call me or just tell me that herself?" She frowned. None of this was making any sense to her. Why would she have to basically go back to the scene of the crime, as it were?

"I wanted to see the infamous Anastasia who drank all the drinks I made that night then destroyed everything in her path." He had a smirk on his beautiful full lips. She wanted to nibble on that bottom lip. Her reaction to him was shocking. The pull towards a man who was a stranger was odd yet exhilarating.

"Wait, you were there that night?"

"Yes, I work for Felipe. I'm the bartender there. My name is Bruno Hunter." He held his hand out to her, and she slowly moved forward and placed her smaller hand into his. The tingles started from where his hand held hers and went straight to her clit. She gulped. *Sex on a fucking stick.*

When he removed his hand from hers, a golden card rested in her hand. She held the card up to her face. It was like the card they'd found in Cinda's room. *Once Upon a Dream Fantasies: Once the door is open all dreams come true. Step inside.*

Quickly she flipped it over. On the other side was the image of two wolves. Two? Two wolves? Her head was spinning, and none of what was happening was making sense other than she knew she had to go get the money she was due and speak to Cinda. Why else would she go there? Lucien. Lucien also worked at the club. The card shimmered with a strange gilded light, and before her eyes the wolves disappeared and her face appeared.

She gasped, her voice hitching and the hand that held the card trembling. "What's this about?"

"Come to the club and find out, Anastasia Trumane."

"I don't think I'm welcomed there." She'd said that more to herself.

"You wouldn't have that card if you weren't."

"I don't think I can go. Tell Cinda I'll get the money from them next month. I don't need it right now." That was the truth, and she was sticking to it. She'd been smart and saved some money. So she didn't have to get the income just yet.

"What a shame. I was hoping to see you there." His eyes were twinkling, and damned if she didn't want to do anything he asked.

"Why'd you want to see me?"

"Why not? Just think about it? There's nothing a few stiff ones can't handle."

Heat filled her face at the imagery those words aroused. His expression let in on the fact that he could tell what she was thinking.

"Drinks, Ana ... I meant drinks."

"Oh, okay. Let me think about it." She licked her lips, and she watched his eyes shift to her mouth.

"You do that, and I'll let you get back to work." Before she could stop him, he'd grabbed her hand and brought it to his lips, kissing the back of it gently, and then he was gone.

She was scared. Not about seeing Cinda, but about going to the club and stepping through the door. There were two wolves there waiting, and she sensed for certain one of those wolves was Lucien.

****

Damn. Lucien was right. With just a touch, he'd wanted to pin Anastasia against the nearest wall and fuck her 'til they were both senseless. She was beautiful, and his desire to take her as well as protect her was high.

When Doc Fairee had approached them with the way to get her back into the club, he'd stated one of them had to go. Bruno had volunteered. Both he and Lucien realized if Luc had shown up that at this point it would send her in the other direction. The wolf in them both wanted her to run, but the human sides knew that this situation demanded finesse. Finesse and a bit of flirt, as Lucien put it; it was everything that Bruno possessed.

Dialing Lucien's number, he waited for him to pick up. He'd promised to report back to him to let him know how it went.

"Talk to me." Fuck, he loved Luc's voice.

"She's perfect for us. She had just the right amount of sass to go along with intelligence."

"That she is. How'd everything go?"

"There's a bit of resistance there, but I think she's intrigued enough to come."

"Tell me you picked up the connection."

"Picked up? Hell, I'm throbbing right now. My wolf doesn't want to play nice."

"Get home." He heard the warning in Lucien's voice. Lucien would understand that his wolf was fighting for dominance to take their mate.

"See you in a few." He hung up the cell and tossed it into the passenger seat.

His hands tightened on the steering wheel as his wolf tried to go back in and claim what it knew belonged to them. It wasn't easy. His wolf almost won out. It wouldn't take anything to go back in and take her. The thought, though delicious and intriguing, wasn't a viable option. *This must be what Lucien has been feeling ever since coming back into contact with Ana.*

What helped him get through was that Bruno was there and able to ease the tension for him. *Fuck, his jeans were tight.* He reached down and adjusted his cock so that he was more comfortable. He had to get home; he needed Lucien in a bad way. Their bond, as with anything, always had to be maintained.

NIKKI PRINCE

Chapter Five

The steam from the shower was working wonders at loosening up the tension running through both of their bodies. Lucien had smelled Ana on Bruno, and they were at each from the minute Bruno had stepped through the doorway.

Lucien drew Bruno close then pushed him up against the tiles facing away from him. Bruno growled his wolf, and Lucien could feel it trying to come to the surface. He growled back.

"Soon we'll have her." Lucien pressed his body into Bruno's, his cock slipping between those perfect ass cheeks. He gave an answering growl.

"It took everything in me to leave."

"I know." He placed kisses on Bruno's shoulders, wrapping one hand to take Bruno's cock in his grasp, he squeezed. The guttural groan that Bruno emitted made Lucien's cock twitch. He slid his hand along that wet shaft and started stroking Bruno firmly. With each pull on Bruno's cock, Lucien bit hard on his shoulder.

"Fuck, you're going to make me spill."

"That's the plan, lover. To make you lose control. Put your hands palm down on the tile." When Bruno would have defied him, Lucien clamped his teeth down onto his shoulder, keeping him in place. Bruno put his hands on the shower wall, if a bit reluctantly.

Releasing his shoulder, he said, "That's it, B. Take what I have to give you."

"Fuck, Lucien. I want you inside me, not your hand jerking me the fuck off."

"You'll get that, soon. Right now … you're going to take everything I give you. We're not going to fuck fully until we have our other mate with us."

"Damn it, you don't play fair, Luc."

"I thought you knew. Who says I'm playing?" He used his other hand to cup Bruno's balls, holding them snugly.

"Fuck me." It was more of a curse than a request.

"Soon, baby, we'll be fucking one another when we have our forever mate with us. Now let go and take what I have to offer in this moment."

Those words from him seemed to push Bruno over the edge, and he was coming hard, his cum coating Lucien's fingers. He squeezed to milk the last drop from him. Bruno grunted and bucked into Lucien's hand.

"That's my boy…" Lucien whispered softly.

Damn, Ana needed to come around and quickly. This jerking each other off was getting tiresome and less satisfying.

****

Drusilla was pacing back and forth in the small hotel room, which seemed to make the place shrink even more. Anastasia watched her from her place on her bed. Drusilla stopped and pointed her finger at her and looked as if she was going to say something, then started pacing again. In her other hand, she had the card that Anastasia had gotten from Bruno.

She'd been debating if she was going to go there, and then this shit happened. Anastasia had been dressing to go to the club after calling and letting them know she was going to be coming. Of course Drusilla was making it hard for her to even get ready to go. The migraines Anastasia had been having of late only seemed to be calmed when she masturbated. What a strange remedy, but it worked. Now she had to deal with this shit from Dru.

"Ana, tell me this isn't what it looks like."

"What does it look like, Dru?"

"It looks like I'm going to have to hunt someone down for messing with my sister."

Anastasia rolled her eyes. "Seriously? What do you mean messing with your sister?"

"That club it isn't your everyday club. You and I both know that just from our visit."

"I know it isn't. This is just for me to go and get my money."

"It seems rather odd yours didn't go in but mine did."

Anastasia shrugged her shoulders. Her sister sounded almost jealous. That couldn't be. Drusilla didn't get jealous, at least not of her, because she always discounted Anastasia. Her sister hadn't said it in so many words, but it hung in the room like the scent of dead cow. The more Dru talked, the angrier Anastasia was getting.

"What the hell is this about, Dru? Why do you have a problem with me going to the club to get my money?"

"Don't you think that Cinda could have done this some other way?"

"She probably could've, but this is where it stands, and I'm going."

"Then I'm going too." Drusilla had stopped her pacing and put both hands on her hips.

"Like hell you are. The invitation to go there was given to me. There's no way I'm going to piss them off again. You're mad you didn't get an invite."

She watched as Drusilla raised her eyebrow and smirked.

"So now this has turned into not only getting your money but also an invitation?"

"After the last time, Dru, do you honestly think I could just walk in there without getting one?"

"It's just mighty odd, that's all."

"Let me have the card, Drusilla. I need it."

Drusilla glanced at the card she held then back up to Anastasia. "What the hell does it mean when it says step inside? Why not just tell you to come by and get your money and go? This looks like more than that."

"I got asked to stop by and get my money. Who knows? Maybe since it's my birthday and Cinda realizes that, she's going to get me a drink or something. The club is a fancy place, as you've seen. So I'll dress up and go get my money. Perhaps a drink or two. That's it, end of story."

"Then ask them if I can come."

"Hell no. You're not going to get me into any more trouble than you have already."

"What do you mean, get you in trouble? Shit, so you're saying all the stuff we've done you didn't want to do?"

"What I'm saying is it's time to grow up. This shit about wanting to get back at Cinda has got to stop."

"Now you're on her side?"

"What the fuck, Drusilla? Are we in high school again? What's this about sides?"

"It's because we're sisters!"

"Right, and no matter the circumstances of how Cinda came to be in our lives, she's our sister now as well. Grow the fuck up."

Drusilla gasped and most certainly if looks could kill Anastasia would have been dead on the spot. With a huff, Drusilla took the card and ripped it down the middle, and then she disdainfully tossed it on the bed, storming out of the hotel room to god knew where. The look she gave Anastasia was one of 'How'd you like that?'

Anastasia was immobile for a bit, staring down at the card, which still shimmered but was in two pieces.

Only Drusilla could be so spiteful. "One of these days, Drusilla Trumane, someone is going to take you to task, and you will not like it, but you will bow down." She said this more to herself, seeing as her sister had left the room and gone off in a little tantrum. She didn't know if she'd be there when it happened, and perhaps it was better she wasn't, but Drusilla Trumane needed to be taken down a peg or two.

She leaned over and picked up the torn card and held it together as if she could put it back together. Why did it hurt that her sister had torn the card? She'd have to take it with her, though she wasn't sure if she needed it; if she did, she wanted to have it. Getting up, she put the card down on the dresser and made her way to the shower.

It was time to get ready. She'd been stalled enough by Drusilla. The place called for club attire, so she'd make sure that's what she had on. It was weird that she had to dress to just get a paycheck, but rules were rules. Dress up she would. Then she'd take Bruno up on that drink and leave as fast as she could. It was her birthday; she didn't want to celebrate it alone. She'd been thinking long and hard about Lucien. If she saw him, she'd just have to be brave and let him know that not under any circumstances did she want to be with him.

God, that little lie hurt. She wanted to be with him in a bad way. The dreams she'd been having were odd in the fact that she had been dreaming of both Luc and Bruno. Why both of them filled her thoughts she didn't know. In her dreams she was with both men in a forest. Lucien was the biggest black wolf she'd ever seen and Bruno a silver one of about the same size.

She'd never been with two men, though the thought didn't bother her. Hell, it was called a ménage and when she'd gone to the club before with Luc in the past there'd been those who practiced that.

The club wasn't just a BDSM club. It was a sex club that catered to everyone's needs. A club that catered to so many fetishes the patrons were bound to be pleased, be that just a couple or more than a couple of people. She'd seen the sex at the tables as well as on the dance floors. It didn't make her feel uncomfortable in the least.

There'd been plenty of times when Lucien had fucked her where she stood, just lifting her dress and taking her. What would it feel like to have Lucien within her and a cock in her mouth? Or in any of her orifices. She chuckled softly. It would be pure heaven she was sure. She sighed at the torrid thought and smiled, thinking it was a shame that it couldn't happen. This was one fantasy that she was sure would never come true, but there was nothing wrong with dreaming a dream.

She didn't want to be late. The shower she took was quick and the makeup she put on light. She'd chosen a red baby doll dress with a neckline that plunged, giving a view of plump breasts yet still enough to tease. It fell above her knees and a pair of red platform shoes finished the ensemble. All this to get a paycheck. She laughed softly. Well, that and perhaps a drink or two. It actually was quite pleasing to dress up again; she'd been just going to work and coming back to the room for too long.

The hairs on the back of her neck began to tingle; glancing quickly at the balcony, she had the oddest sensation that someone was watching her. But that was insane. The room was on the second floor, which was high enough for it to be silly to think someone was there watching her. Yet, she couldn't shake the feeling. Maybe she was more tired than she thought. Moving away from the armoire where she was adding the finishing touches to her makeup, she strolled over to the window and opened it.

Peering out into the darkness, she didn't see anything until a flash of movement caught the corner of her eye and she leaned forward on the balcony, holding on to the rail. What appeared to be two big dogs ran through the dimly lit parking lot below and off into the trees. Dogs? No, they were too big to be dogs. Those were wolves.

She must be going mad.

NIKKI PRINCE

Chapter Six

Lucien looked over at Bruno as they crouched, both in their full wolf forms, near the edge of the thick line of trees that bordered the parking lot. It had been a close one, but both had been so enraptured at seeing Anastasia they'd risked it all. So in lust they almost got caught by her. Love and want made one foolish. The one thing that made them breathe easier was the knowledge she was going to go to the club. Bruno's silver coat shone in the mottled moonlight while Lucien's ebony fur blended completely.

Let's just take her. Bruno the wolf stood and made as if to go back to the balcony where Ana still stood looking out in their general direction, and with a snarl the black wolf moved in front of the silver one.

No, now is not the time. We will have her soon enough. He bared his teeth, showing his dominance.

We've waited long enough! The silver wolf whined.

Yes, and we will have her at the club. Now come!

Bruno's yellowish eyes spoke volumes, and with a low growl Lucien nudged him and pushed him back into the trees. It was time to claim their mate. No time to lose, he went into a run with Bruno fast on his heels. They had to make it to the club before Ana.

****

Anastasia sat in a backroom at a table of the club, legs crossed and hands on her knees. She was about to start getting impatient. *Why was she being made to wait?* If they were just giving her her money, there wasn't any reason to do this. *Where was Cinda?* She'd thought there wasn't a reason to be scared or nervous around Cinda. Truth be told, she was damn nervous. She owed her sister an apology. Maybe Cinda didn't want to see her again. Maybe she'd be sending in her man, Nico Charming, to give her the money. Either way, at the moment she wished the earth would just swallow her up and take her.

This was almost like going to grandma's house and getting in trouble. The wait was excruciatingly painful. She'd been there for almost thirty minutes when the door opened. Cinda entered with Nico and sat down at the table in front of her.

Cinda was dressed suggestively in a leather skirt and corset, and she'd never looked hotter or happier to Anastasia. Cinda placed a big box with a red bow on the table. She'd been so busy admiring how Cinda looked that she hadn't noticed the box 'til now.

"What's that?" Anastasia couldn't help but ask. She'd always been a curious person. Her grandmother used to always tell her that her curiosity went above and beyond.

"You'll find out once we've had a little talk," Cinda said. The direct mien Cinda gave her made Anastasia squirm.

"Okay." It was all she could say. She was so nervous, and she didn't want to say anything stupid.

"Ana, as long as we've been sisters, we've never just talked straight with each other. That isn't only your fault; I take responsibility for that as well." When Anastasia would've said something, Cinda raised her hand.

"No, let me finish. I want you to hear what I have to say." She cleared her throat, and Anastasia could tell that she was struggling to find the right words.

"When my mother died and daddy told me that I was going to get a new mother and sisters, I was elated. I'd always wanted sisters." Anastasia watched as Nico put his arm around Cinda's shoulders, a true sign of comforting.

"For a little while, it worked. We were all one happy family, and I don't know what happened to make it change. I don't know if I just fantasized the whole thing and it wasn't how it really was, or if something I did changed it. Your mother seemed to change on me and then the two of you did. After they died, I wanted to close the gap, but it seemed too late. I want to ask your forgiveness."

"Forgiveness for what, Cinda? I mean, you're right. We were horrible to you and so was mother. If anyone should ask for forgiveness, it should be me and Dru." She shook her head in disbelief that Cinda could be asking for forgiveness.

"The reason I want to ask for forgiveness is there were plenty of times that I could've at least tried to speak with the two of you. I didn't. Therein lies my culpability." Cinda's eyes teared up. Nico gave her a handkerchief, and she dabbed at her eyes.

"Oh, I see. You're forgiven, of course, Cinda, and I wanted to speak with you tonight to ask for forgiveness as well. The plain and simple truth of the matter is that my mother was jealous of the affection your father placed on you, and her ugliness about that situation wore off on us."

Cinda paused for a moment after Anastasia stopped talking, seeming to search for what she wanted to say.

"I'm sorry. So many times I wanted to say something as well, but I was following Drusilla. That's another thing I'm guilty of and sorry for. Please forgive me. I know we haven't been close, and we may never be as close as we could have been. I'd like to at least remedy that and forge a better relationship." She reached over to cover Cinda's hand with her own. "Please forgive me."

Cinda covered Anastasia's hand with her own and nodded her head. She was now crying as well. They held hands for a few moments longer, both women crying. God, she'd been so blind. Her loyalty had been misplaced, and she'd wasted so much time.

"I forgive you, Ana. It will be nice to have a sister at last. Who knows, perhaps Drusilla will come around, and we can all at least have one another."

"Thank you, Cinda."

Cinda stood and came around the table and held her arms out. Anastasia couldn't hold back the big grin that she knew was on her face as she moved into Cinda's arms and hugged her tight. They clung to one another, both of them tucking their faces into the other's neck. Cinda pulled back after a moment, holding Anastasia by her arms.

"Now I did want to wish you a happy birthday. My gift to you is what's in that box. You can walk away now, or you can take it. As the card said, 'step through the door'. Even if you don't, your paycheck is in the envelope inside, and you can walk away with that. But you can't open the box here. You will need to take it up to the suite I've reserved for your birthday."

What on earth could possibly be in that box? It all seemed so mysterious. Why couldn't Cinda just tell her?

"Wow, a suite?" She clapped her hands in excitement. "After sharing a hotel room with Dru, this is going to be nice!" Cinda, Nico, and Anastasia all laughed. The tension had dissipated from the room, and Anastasia had never sensed she was home more than she did now.

Cinda leaned forward and kissed her cheek.

"See you soon. Don't be a stranger. Dante will lead you to the suite. He's waiting just outside the door. Oh and yeah, don't open the box until you're inside the suite."

With that said they left, with Nico's arms wrapped securely around Cinda's waist. *To find something like that would be wonderful. The love was just pouring off of them.* The next question on her mind was whether or not she wanted to find out what was in the box. The answer to that was hell fucking yeah.

Grabbing the box, she opened the door and spoke to the only person standing next to the door.

"Dante, I presume?"

"Yes, ready to go to the suite?"

"Lead the way."

He took the package from her and offered his arm. Looping her arm into his, she matched her gait to his. Whatever was in the box and inside the suite, she was ready for a change.

NIKKI PRINCE

Chapter Seven

She had butterflies in the pit of her stomach and by the time they'd stopped at the room, after weaving through half naked patrons and full on naked patrons, her body was warm with need. Wasn't that just the way? Hell, before the night was through she'd have to find someone for herself.

Dante opened the door and stood to the side; she took the gift box from him and thanked him as she entered. He shut the door behind her, and she heard a soft click of the lock. She was being locked in? For a moment, she was worried. Then she shrugged that off. Cinda wouldn't harm her. It was to keep others from coming in.

She stopped in the middle of the room, admiring it. The walls had been painted so that it looked like a forest; the canopy bed in the middle of the room was large and had coverings on top that looked functional. The ceiling was all glass, along with a tall mirror by the dresser.

The furniture was all done in beautiful cherry wood and the coverings in rich chocolate and gold accents. The room also had a really cozy feeling to it. There was a dresser, a closet, what she assumed was a bathroom door and another door that looked like a connecting room. Cinda had gone all out with giving her a birthday gift. Damn.

There was also a balcony that she assumed faced the back of the building, as the front of the building looked like a warehouse to her and nothing special. It was amazing what was hidden within. She set the box down on the bed and stared at it. Did she want to see what she'd been given? What could it hurt?

She leisurely untied the bow, letting it rest at the sides of the large box, and opened it, setting the lid on the bed. Inside was an envelope like Cinda had said. But under it was tissue paper that was obscuring what else was in the box. She picked up the envelope, opening it and seeing her check within. She almost put it down until she noted there was another piece of paper inside, a handwritten note addressed to her.

Dear Anastasia Trumane,

We're going to play a little game. Try this on for size. We think it will fit, perfectly. We will be coming for you in 30 minutes. Get dressed and wait for us on the bed.

Anonymously Yours.

Cinda had arranged for her to play at the club! The note also indicated more than one person. She gave a girly giggle of excitement and peeled back the tissue paper. She gasped. The fabric was exquisite, soft and utterly sensual.

She took each item out of the box. There was a bra top with a brooch clasp, a sheer flowing cape, and a long skirt with a slit up its side and built-in boy shorts. It was the sexiest ensemble she'd ever seen, and it was all in red. How perfect this outfit would go with the shoes she wore.

She had less than twenty minutes to get ready. *Time to put up or shut up.* She'd wanted to have something happen. Well, it was happening. She stripped as fast as she could then put on the costume. *Little Red Riding Hood never looked this good.* She hung her clothing up inside the closet and pirouetted in front of the mirror.

So this was what it could be like, not to be under Drusilla's thumb or her mother's. But doing something she wanted for her, something wild and out of the ordinary. She was sexy hot. She stroked a hand along her uncovered thigh and smiled.

The slit accentuated her long legs and the top pushed her breasts up in offering to whomever wished to partake. Naughty and beautiful, those were the words she'd use to describe herself. She arranged her long curls over her shoulders and put on the hood that was attached to the cape. One last glance in the mirror and she went to the bed, hopped up on it and positioned herself in the middle and then waited for what was to come.

She observed the door, wondering who'd step through. There was a sound of a door opening, but it wasn't the front door. It was the adjoining room. Dante stood there, nodded to her and then exited. For a moment she thought it was him, but that couldn't be.

Not that he wasn't attractive but...

Her thought trailed off as she stared at the door. She was frozen in place.

She gasped. Two wolves, two very large wolves entered the room. One was black in color; the other was silver, and they were huge. Someone closed the door, she assumed Dante. That spurred her into action, and she jumped over the other side of the bed trying to reach the door. The silver wolf blocked her path, and when she tried to run to the other door, the black one blocked her way.

Don't be afraid, Red. Lucien, it was Lucien.

"Stop this, Luc, let me go." Oh my god! Wait a fucking minute, she could hear him. She could understand everything he was saying, and he was a wolf. "How can I understand you?" She could hear the alarm in her own voice.

You're our mate. Of course you can understand everything we say. As our mate, you can hear our thoughts and feel when we are hurt. The only way you wouldn't be able to is if we are too far away or if we are blocking the thoughts from you. Stay and play awhile with us.

"No, I don't want to." She backed up against the bed when Lucien advanced on her. He nuzzled her legged and growled softly.

Of course you want to. I can smell how wet you are. Let us love you.

"I need to go." Still they blocked her path.

Ana, my girl, if you go, the headaches will continue. In fact, they will get worse.

"How do you know I've been having headaches?"

We all have. Our pain will only build if we don't complete our mating match. So long ago, when you and I were together, you became my mate. I didn't realize what it fully meant.

"Mating match? Lucien, you're making no sense. Besides, there is the little detail of you being here with someone else, not just me. Are you going to tell me this is all because you're both my mates?"

Yes. Though not only are you my mate, he's my mate as well. That admission didn't shock her, and Lucien would be privy to that fact. When they'd been together, Lucien had point blank told her he was bisexual.

"Lucien, if this is your way of trying to get me back into your bed." She gasped as she was hit with the most excruciating pain between her eyes. She brought her hand to her forehead and held it.

Lucien, hurry.

Anastasia turned to look at the other wolf, who'd come closer to them, and she was now hearing what he was saying in her mind. When she turned back to Lucien, he'd shifted and stood before her naked.

"You're everything I imagined you to be." That voice, she recognized that voice. It was Bruno. Her eyes widened as that beautiful male specimen stood next to her.

"Bruno." He'd shifted as well and was in all his naked glory.

"Yes, Red, my dear, I'm your other wolf," Bruno stated gruffly.

Lucien placed his hands around her waist while she was distracted, and she moaned softly. It had been too long since she'd received a strong man's touch.

"Lucien..." She whimpered. His blue eyes twinkled.

He was giving her a chance to stop him. The one thing he'd always told her was that she had the right to refuse him, to tell him she didn't want to go forward. He was a Dom who didn't do the safe word thing; all she had to do to stop him was to say no. She couldn't say no; truthfully, she didn't wish to say no.

When she didn't say anything, he spoke again.

"Let us ease your pain," Lucien persuaded.

Lucien pulled her into the center of the room, and Bruno pressed behind her. She could feel both of their cocks against her, and she trembled. One against her stomach, the other against her ass. There were two hard cocks, two wolves for her to have. Why not live the fantasy and play along?

"Our little Red," Bruno mumbled and then nipped the back of her neck. Her legs almost buckled.

"My, what beautiful eyes you both have," she said with a tongue-in-cheek grin.

If they wanted to play as if she was Red Riding Hood, she'd play.

"Better to see you with, Red," rumbled Lucien, who'd buried his face between her breasts. He was taking deep breaths, drawing her in.

"Mmm … what strong arms you both have," Anastasia answered back.

"All the better to hold on tight to you, my sweet Red, and to never let you go." This time it was Lucien who spoke.

She dropped her head back onto Bruno's shoulders as hands—she wasn't sure whom they belonged to—cupped her breasts and pulled at the nipples. She groaned and arched into the hands on her breasts.

"Oh my, what nice legs you have."

"All the better to help us push into you, my dear Red," growled Bruno.

She gasped in protest when both men suddenly moved away from her. Her eyes fluttered open.

Lucien drew her close, kissing her hard, and then slipping his tongue inside of her mouth. He claimed every part of her mouth as his. She mewled as her ass cheeks were parted, and Bruno nipped each cheek in turn before running his tongue over her puckered little hole, rimming it. She jerked in surprise but not because it didn't feel good. It did—it felt too damn good.

Red, I'm going to be the one to claim you first. I started this process. Bruno will claim you next. Then we will both claim that beautiful ass of yours at some point. Do you understand?

She whimpered as his words filtered through to her, and then the bite to her bottom lip shot thrills throughout her entire body. She was so wet it was coating her thighs. *My god, they want every inch of me.*

Lucien took his lips from hers, and then picked her up, carrying her to the bed. He deposited her at the edge of it, pushing her legs open. He knelt in front of her, his intent obvious. The first swipe of his tongue against her clit sent shockwaves through her body. All she could think was it had been too long.

"My, what a wicked mouth you have," she said to Lucien.

"All the better to eat you with, my dear." He gave a long lick to her clit and sucked it into his mouth. Unable to help herself, she started rocking into his hot mouth.

The bed sank, and Bruno moved behind her. He took off her hood, pulled her hair until her head fell back, and then he was giving her one of the hottest kisses ever. The sting of that pull only made her want more. She loved it rough. Lucien must have told him. *Boy, these two men could kiss.* He thrust his tongue deeper, licking every inch of her mouth. He kept one hand tangled in her hair. *Fuck, kisses to her clit and kisses to her mouth. What more could a woman ask for?*

NIKKI PRINCE

Chapter Eight

By the time Bruno stopped kissing her, she and he were both breathing extremely hard. He moved to the side of her, cupping the back of her head with one hand and his cock with the other. It was huge and beautiful, the bulbous head leaking his pre-cum. *Fuck.* He looked to be about eight inches and the girth, good god. She wasn't sure she could do it as she stared at it. The choice was taken from her when he pulled her towards his cock. She knew what he wanted, and she would do it gladly.

Don't worry, my sweet Ana. Take what you can. I will hold on to the rest if need be.

Tentatively, she licked over the top of it, sliding her tongue along the pearly essence that had formed at the slit. She heard him groan, the hand that was tangled in hair tightening painfully.

"Take more of me in, baby."

Lucien took her legs and wrapped them around his shoulders then pressed his face into her, dipping his tongue into her wet slit. He swirled two fingers into her entrance, teasing her. She bucked forward, trying to ride his fingers.

"Uh uh, Red. I will fuck you when I'm ready to fuck you. Take what I give you and suck our boy's cock."

Obediently she took more of his cock in her mouth, sucking the head and running her tongue around the crest then slowly taking as much of him in as she could. He pumped his cock at the base with his hand; she had no need to worry about him falling from her mouth. He was feeding her his cock.

"Damn, Lucien, she sucks like a fucking pro."

"That she does, Bruno. Her mouth was made for fucking." She warmed at their praise. Once again she found herself trying to ride Luc's fingers, which were curved against her g-spot. She wanted more, but to her horror Luc removed his fingers and Bruno took his cock from her mouth. They both moved away, and feeling confused, she scrutinized them both.

"What, what's wrong?" She couldn't take it any longer and had to ask.

They ignored her, and Lucien turned to Bruno.

"B, go pull out the spanking horse. I think our girl needs to learn to listen."

Anastasia gulped, her eyes going wide as Bruno strolled towards the closet. The spanking chair, she remembered him having one at his condo, and there had been several times she'd ended up strapped to it. Some things never change. Bruno went into the adjoining room and came out with the chair, and her pussy moistened even more.

"Look at me, Red," Lucien ordered.

It was then she noticed he'd grabbed a flogger from only god knew where. She'd been so busy watching for Bruno to return. He ran the flogger over her cheek, and then stroked it over her breasts all the while his eyes stayed on hers.

"Take the skirt off. Keep the shoes on and the top on. Then go to Bruno and get strapped in."

The spanking that was coming was a lesson for her, and it was also Lucien's way of giving her a consequence for not listening. Getting off the bed, she undid her skirt and then slipped it down her hips. She stepped out of it and put it on the bed. The next thing was her cape; undoing the tie, she tossed the cape to the bed right alongside the skirt. She wasted no time in getting to Bruno, who'd set up the sawhorse in the middle of the room.

Anastasia straddled the chair face down, and Bruno secured her to it.

"Damn, Luc, what a fine ass she has."

"Mhm, I'm going to flog her 'til it's nice and red and burning hot." There was a squeeze to her ass cheek, and she hummed in pleasure. The flogging would hurt, but the pain and pleasure would mix so well. It had been a long while since she'd had this done.

"She looks eager, Lucien."

"I'm sure she is. Though it hurts and she usually cries, the pleasure she gains and the lesson she learns make it all the better."

"Oh really now?" Bruno said.

"Isn't that right, Red?" Lucien tapped her ass lightly with the flogger.

"Oh! Yes, you're right, Luc." They were an unconventional dominant and submissive. Just because she didn't call him sir or master didn't mean he wasn't those things to her.

"Why do you think I'm spanking you, Ana?"

There was a hand in her hair, stroking lightly. Bruno.

"It's because I tried to fuck myself on your fingers when you told me not to, Lucien."

The flogger came down with a solid sting to her left cheek, and she lurched against the straps with a soft groan.

"Exactly, Red. Your ass is going to be as red as your hair when I'm done, but you'll listen, won't you?" She was given another stinging slap with the flogger to her right cheek.

She hissed through the pain. "Mmm, yes, I'll listen."

It seemed to be all he needed to hear as he stopped talking and pounded her ass. By the end, her ass was stinging with a painful pleasure that had tears streaking her cheeks. Lucien rubbed his hand against her ass in small circles.

"When I give a command, what must follow?"

"My utter obedience, Luc."

"Do I have that now from you?"

She nodded her head, though she made sure to speak as well. "Yes, always yes."

Her ass cheeks were spread. The coolness of lube drizzled down on her puckered hole, and she sighed. The swirl of his fingers against her there made her moan. He teased around the hole then dipped one finger inside her sphincter, turning it this way and that as he readied her to take one of their cocks. She grunted as he pushed in all the way to the knuckle then withdrew to the tip. The next moment she felt full as he added a second finger, allowing her to get used to being stretched.

"Move back against my fingers. Fuck them."

Eager to please him, she did just as he asked, wiggling back into his fingers so that she was fucking herself on them. She pushed back against him for a few moments more before he tapped her ass lightly with his free hand and then slid his fingers out of her.

"Perfect, you're nice and loose. Since you've been such a good girl, I'm going to forgo prolonging your need for cock. Bruno, free her."

The more commands Lucien gave out, the hotter she was getting and from the looks of it, Bruno didn't mind being led around by Luc either.

"It's time we take our mate. There is time to play later on."

Lucien's voice was gruff. She could tell that he was just as ready to fuck as she was to have them fuck her. In no time Bruno had her free and cradled in his arms. She nuzzled his neck, and she felt the rumbling of his chest. She was on fire, and she wanted them both right now. This was all in Lucien's time.

"You're a tease, little Red," Bruno stated.

"Yes, Luc didn't tell you that?" She nipped his neck, and he hissed.

He sat her on her feet in front of the bed, where Lucien already stood. She noticed the two foil wrappers within his hands. She blinked and was about to question why when Lucien spoke.

"No matter what we are, we can still get you pregnant. Now is not the time for that. We are just learning one another again. You and Bruno are new to one another. You're very fertile."

She gasped. "How do you know that?"

Lucien tapped his nose and smirked. "We're wolves."

"Oh." How foolish of her, the whole sense of smell thing.

There was nothing like being protected by a lover, but to have two men who wanted you and were willing to take that extra care was priceless.

Lucien held out both condoms to her, and he and Bruno sat down on the bed.

"You do the honors, my sweet Red."

Both men's dicks were standing at perfect attention, both thick and long. Lucien's was curved and Bruno's ramrod straight. She touched her lips to make sure she wasn't drooling. How embarrassing that would be. She chuckled softly.

"My, what beautiful cocks you have."

"All the better to fuck you with, my dear," Lucien said, and she smiled as he winked at her.

Kneeling down in front of them, she set one condom on Luc's leg and opened the other. The crinkle of the foil packet opening filled the room. She placed the condom on the tip of Lucien's dick and slowly rolled it down. She couldn't help but giggle at the thought that ran through her head.

"Pray tell, may I ask what's so funny?" Lucien asked, putting his hand under her chin and pulling her head up so they were eye to eye.

"Just thinking about the old saying a wolf in sheep's clothing. The condoms you bought are lambskin." Both men chuckled with her.

"Luc, may I ask how you'll be able to claim me if you're wearing condoms?"

She'd finished putting the condom on him and now moved between Bruno's thighs to cover him with his. Lucien took her hand once she was done and made her rise.

"Claiming isn't only in the fucking. It will also be your receiving our bite at the same time during penetration."

"I'm ready for it."

"You may think you're ready for it right now, but it's going to hurt. Once our DNA fully fuses with your body and is in your system, it will hurt. There is no way around that pain, my sweet."

"If I'm to be your mate as well as Bruno's, there's no way around it anyway."

"Brave girl," Bruno said.

Nodding, Lucien moved to the bed, lying flat on his back with his legs dangling over the edge feet flat on the floor. "Come climb on me, and take me inside."

Eagerness didn't begin to describe how she was feeling. She straddled him, rising so that she could grasp his cock. She bit back a moan, rubbing his cock against her entrance. She was aching and only being filled with cock would she be complete again. Lucien's hands went to her waist so that he was steadying her. Finally having her balance, she slid down on to his cock 'til he was as deep as he could go.

"That's my girl; now make me nice and wet."

NIKKI PRINCE

Chapter Nine

There was nothing quite like having him within her again. She'd missed it. There was a push to her back, and she moved forward, pressing her chest to Lucien's. Rolling her hips, she intended to make it nice and wet for them all. He countered each of her moves, both of them grinding together.

Bruno wasn't idle at all; the squirting sound of lube filled the room and then the sticky coolness of that lube being liberally applied to her ass told her of Bruno's intentions. Their goal was double penetration. The next sensation was of Bruno stroking his fingers over her ass once again to prepare her. He wasn't small by any means. They were going to stuff her full.

Lucien caught her attention by gripping her hair in his hand and tugging hard. She hissed in pleasure. He brought her mouth to his and gave her a hard kiss, nipping and licking at her lips. The bites were hard and added a pleasurable sting.

****

Damn. He thought he'd watch for a bit but fuck if he could. Bruno stood there as long as he could, then he grabbed the lube and started to lube her up. His cock was hurting he needed to fuck her so badly. She was nice and stretched, and now he was going to take her. Dropping the lube on the bed, he took his cock in one hand and spread her ass with the other.

He pushed the tip of his cock into her ass, trying to take it slow until he heard her grunt and felt her push back into him, drawing him past the tight ring of muscles and deep inside of her.

"Ahh." He put his hands just belong Lucien's on her waist and stood there between Luc's legs.

Anastasia gave a deep moan, and he could feel her body shuddering for a bit before she regained herself. Lucien groaned and started thrusting inside of Ana even faster.

"Fuck her, Bruno," Lucien urged.

It was all he needed to hear his man tell him to fuck their girl. He thrust into her slowly at first and then he sped up, moving to the same rhythm that they were setting. The slide of his cock inside of her also gave him the pleasure of the sensation of Lucien's cock rubbing against his own. Fantastic.

"It's time, Ana and Bruno," he heard Lucien say.

His inner wolf howled, and Lucien's gave an answering howl. Time to claim their mate. Lucien was far ahead of him, laying claim to her right shoulder with his mouth, teeth lengthening. Bruno leaned down to bite the other shoulder, extending his fangs as well.

****

Anastasia let out a loud scream as both pairs of fangs bit into her shoulder. The pain was unlike anything she'd ever felt. There came a point when the pain from the bites fused into pleasure, and a burning sensation surrounded each bite, followed by uncontrollable lust and the need to mate with them. Every molecule in her body hummed with excitement. She could actually hear the blood running through her veins, not only her veins but also theirs. Their hearts synched and beat together, as one. Nothing had ever felt so right, so good and so unspoiled.

It was like scales had been ripped from her eyes, and only now could she see clearly. See them as they truly were; see their wolves and humans standing side by side. Lucien and Bruno, her mates. They were hers as much as she was theirs. They were bonded, bonded as closely as anyone could ever be, and it was unbreakable.

They kept their fangs imbedded in her shoulder for what seemed like an eternity. Once she was released from the bites, both men licked over where their teeth had just been. Bruno pressed his head into her back, trailing kisses on her shoulder blades and licking her skin.

"Oh fuck, fuck me harder." She all but begged them. How could she have ever thought she didn't need Lucien? Hell, now she needed Bruno just as much.

Sweat was dripping from her body; she didn't care, and it wasn't time to look pretty. It was time to get fucked by her mates. She heard Lucien roar and then he was rending her top from her body, freeing her breasts. Her breasts bounced wildly as they fucked, and she alternated between squeezing her cunt muscles around Lucien's cock and her inner ass muscles around Bruno's cock.

"Let go, both of you, fucking let go and come with me!"

Lucien's voice was harsh, the mandate pushing her over the edge into orgasmic oblivion. She gushed, her cream soaking Lucien and Bruno in turn. Lucien's and Bruno's shouts blanketed the room. Heavy breathing took over as they tried to regain their composure. Her body was moist with sweat from herself and her men. It was a grand sensation.

She hadn't realized she'd drifted off a bit until Bruno lifted from them and pulled out. She whimpered because she was sore but in a good way. Lucien kissed her shoulders where they'd both bitten her then gave her ass a pat. There was a sound of a door opening, and she could only assume that Bruno had gone into the bathroom.

"Such a good girl."

A cool, wet cloth touched her ass, and Bruno began cleansing her gently. Lucien's hands rubbed up and down her back, soothing her. She almost fell asleep once more until Bruno pulled her up into his arms and off Lucien's cock. She grumbled in protest.

"Now, now, Red, I'm just going to lay you down on the bed so you can rest while I clean our dearest Lucien."

She nodded and lay back against the pillows where he'd set her. She was propped up and would be able to see everything that went on. She wanted to watch Lucien and Bruno in action. Bruno took the condom off of Lucien and tossed it into the trash next to the bed. He then took a cloth and cleansed Luc's semi-hard dick. In fascination she watched Luc's cock jerk and come back to life, hardening in Bruno's hand. Her legs started to tremble, and there was a rush of something she couldn't define running through her body. White-hot need. Panting hard, she held her legs together as her pussy began to throb.

"So soon? I thought I was going to rest," she said before she could stop the words.

Lucien, who was still lying down, turned his head to assess her. A gentle smile on his lips as Bruno cared for him. "Yes, right now there are hormones running through your body because of our mating. It's forcing you into heat."

"Heat? But I'm not a werewolf."

"Very true, but you're a werewolf's mate. In fact, you have a double whammy; you belong to me and to Bruno. The same thing you're going through we are as well. We're just a bit better at dealing with it."

She inhaled a big gulp of air when Bruno stopped cleaning Lucien only to take his cock into his mouth, sucking on him as if he was sucking a lollypop. He took him all the way in his mouth. Lucien's hand went to cup

Bruno's head, and his other hand stroked gently along her leg.

"Come here, Red. Straddle my face; I want a taste of your sweet pussy while B keeps me nice and hard."

She was more than eager to do what he asked and quickly she straddled his face, resting most of her weight against his chest. Lucien took her waist into his hands and pulled her flush against his mouth, burying his face between her folds as he licked roughly. She heard little mewling sounds and grasped that she was making those noises.

Lucien played with her clit like he was playing the violin, string by glorious string. She rolled her hips so that she was riding his face as if she were riding his cock. He moved his hands to cup her ass and grind her into his mouth.

She glanced back at Bruno, who was now stroking Lucien's cock with his hand and had his face down between his legs, licking and sucking on Lucien's balls. She licked her lips, as her mouth was suddenly dry from the view.

"Make Lucien come, Bruno. I want to feel his cum spray against my body."

She yelped as Lucien smacked her ass and pulled on her clit.

"You naughty girl," Lucien said after lifting his head away from her for a moment.

"Mmm, yes ... now, please ... we both want your cum. Isn't that right, Bruno?"

"Oh yes, she's right. Come for me and Red, Luc."

Anastasia reached back to take a hold of Lucien's cock, helping Bruno jerk him off. Bruno pushed Lucien's legs up, giving Lucien a rim job. *Wonderful.* Bruno was on the same page and was going to help her get him off and fast. Lucien cried out and came in sticky white jets that hit his lower belly and chest, as well as her back and buttocks.

"Now that's how you get your mate off..." Anastasia said with a purr.

Chapter Ten

They were all extremely satiated, having fucked each other in varying positions. Lucien fucking Bruno, Bruno fucking Ana; it had all been done and was all fantastic. He looked up as a shadow fell over the table.

"There's a commotion at the front door, Lucien." Flora had come over to their table while they were eating dinner at the club. They needed to refuel after coming up for air from their time in the suite. He'd also promised her a cake for her birthday. Apparently that would have to wait.

He frowned, as he found it odd that he'd be interrupted from his fantasy time for commotion at the door when he wasn't working as a guard. That alone told him it was something that concerned him. Flora leaned in close to him and whispered softly into his ear. She was never one to scream or shout, but she had her own commanding air. A Domme that no one ever thought was one until they locked swords with her.

The commotion turned out to be fucking Drusilla Trumane making problems outside the front door. *Fuck a duck. She couldn't leave well enough alone.* When rebuffed at the front door and told she wasn't allowed in, she'd stayed outside ranting and raving. Several of the customers had complained that she'd even bothered them as they came in or tried to leave.

Ana was sitting in Bruno's lap and having a conversation with him. His first thought was to take care of Drusilla himself, but then what benefit would come from that for Ana? This was a demon she needed to slay herself. Though she was his, there were some things that she must do for herself. This was Ana's opportunity, and she needed to be the one who told Drusilla to either fuck off or fly straight.

"Thank you, Flora. Please escort Drusilla Trumane to my suite. Give her a glass of wine on the house and tell her to wait."

"What should I tell her about her sister?"

"Tell her that she will be along shortly. Please stand watch in the room. She's a hellion."

Flora grinned, her green eyes twinkling, and she all but purred in his ear.

"I love hellions. They're quite fun to tame. Don't worry. I will enjoy this."

Lucien turned away from Flora and watched as Bruno whispered something in Ana's ear and she giggled. Anastasia's expression changed when she looked at him. She gave him the most sensual looking smile he'd yet to see on her face. That look connected with his wolf, and he felt the beast within calm. His wolf all at once saw that no matter what happened she was there to stay with them. She blew him a kiss then went back to her conversation with Bruno. She was distracted, which was a good thing. He'd talk to Bruno and get things into motion with Ana.

Bruno, Drusilla is here and has requested to see Ana. Bruno's stare met his over the top of Ana's head, and the slight nod he gave let in on the fact that Bruno understood the brevity of the situation for Ana. *Send her over to me. Please, I'd like you to go and make sure that Drusilla gets settled in. You don't have to be in the room with her. Flora will do that.*

Yes, if anyone can keep Drusilla in line, it would be Flora.

Bruno nodded and kissed the top of her head, then set her on her feet, nudging her over to Lucien. Standing, Bruno took off with a confident stroll towards the suite. Ana paused only to watch as Bruno left, a small frown on her face as she settled in Lucien's lap.

"Where's Bruno going off to in such a hurry? Why does it feel like something is wrong?"

"Kiss me first."

She leaned in and kissed him, not your everyday peck either. No, she kissed him full on, thrusting her tongue into his mouth. Her frown was gone.

That's my girl. He tugged her lips from his with a subtle pull of her hair.

"Now, Bruno is heading back to the suite, as we've had a little situation arise."

He kissed her forehead, and then waited to see if she'd realize what the issue was and how it connected to her. She looked towards the suite again then back at him.

"Drusilla's here, isn't she? Who's with her?"

"Yes, and she wants to see you, but she came alone. Are you ready for that? Flora's with her. She can take anything that Drusilla may try to dish out. As bubbly as Flora is, she's also a Domme and a very good one."

Anastasia sat up straight in his lap and nodded. "If I'm to be with you and Bruno, I have to get over my past. I'm hoping that Drusilla will want to be part of my new future. If she doesn't, I can't worry about that. I can't let her continue to make me or anyone else I love miserable."

He stroked his thumb over her bottom lip. "We'll discuss the L word when this mess with Drusilla is over. Now come, grab one of the robes when we get by the desk and throw it on. I know you want Drusilla to understand, but shocking her into it right now isn't the right way. Though I do think she needs a flogging."

Ana giggled and kissed the corner of his mouth and then bounded off his lap. He held out his hand to her when he stood and led her away from their table. When they passed the front desk, she grabbed a purple robe and pulled it on, tying it together. He grabbed one as well.

Though he wasn't planning to go in, he didn't know if he'd have to. When they reached the suite, Bruno was waiting by the door in a robe with his arms crossed over his chest.

Bruno reached over and cupped Ana's cheek. "You sure you want to do this?"

"Yes. If I don't, there isn't any closure."

Bruno and Lucien both gave her a soft kiss.

"Thank you both. Don't worry, I'll be fine." Ana moved past them both, opened the door and went in, closing it softly.

"Let's go get a drink," Lucien said.

"You think she'll be okay?"

"I know she will be. Our wolves chose her for a reason. If she were weak, they wouldn't want her."

"Right. Yes, I want a beer."

"She'll let us know if she needs us."

"True, now how about we see who can drink the most shots while we wait?" Bruno's lopsided grin showed Lucien that his boy was going to be okay with what was happening.

"Yes, let's."
****

Some things were going to change, Anastasia thought. Her sister couldn't keep interrupting her life like this. Flora was standing in the room, her hands on her hips as she walked back and forth in front of a very tied up Drusilla. *What on earth?* There was red bondage tape holding Drusilla's wrists together and her ankles as well as she sat in a chair in the middle of the room. She also had a ball gag on her mouth.

"Wow, did I miss something, Flora?"

Flora was grinning from ear to ear. The corset and skirt she wore were beautiful black leather and accompanied by extremely high heels. The petite dynamo loved her heels.

"Nothing I couldn't handle. Your sister dared me to do it."

Drusilla looked furious and yet at the same time something else Anastasia couldn't quite define was in those brown eyes. Her hair was messed up, and her lipstick looked a bit smeared. Interesting.

"She dared you to gag her and tie her up?"

"Yes. I brought her in here, and she thought that she could command me about. I told her if anyone was going to take orders it would be her taking them from me. I also told her if she didn't stop the back talk I'd have her tied and gagged."

"Well, I can tell she didn't listen." She couldn't stop the chuckle that tumbled from her lips. Drusilla glared at her and made grunting sounds beneath the ball gag.

"Drusilla, my dear, you need me to keep it on you a bit longer?" Flora said in her cheerful voice. Drusilla glared, but she quieted down again.

"Thank you, Flora. I need to talk to my sister."

"Gotcha, call for me if you need me." With a sway of her hips, Flora exited the room and closed the door softly behind her.

She put her attention back on Dru. "Okay, do I need to keep the ball gag in, or will you talk like you have some sense? Nod your head yes if you can do the latter."

Drusilla was still glaring, but she nodded. Before she went to her sister to remove the gag, she retrieved the other chair in the room and placed it in front of Drusilla's. That done, she removed the gag from Dru's mouth. Dru moved her mouth around as if she was yawning. Anastasia waited to let her adjust to not being gagged.

Chapter Eleven

"How dare you let that woman do this to me!" Drusilla started in immediately, and Anastasia shook her head.

"Shut up, Dru. This is my birthday and my time. You came here and disturbed me. So now you will listen and talk when it's your turn."

Drusilla gasped, and the look on her face was comical.

"That's better." Anastasia crossed her legs and paused for a moment.

Now she reflected on the right things to say to Drusilla, to get off of her chest what she should have a long time ago to her sister so there could truly be closure, at least on her end.

"I love you, Dru. You're my sister." She sighed. "The way we've been going on is wrong. We missed out on a great opportunity to have someone else to care for when we decided to take up mom's crusade against Cinda."

"What are you talking about? That's our mom's memory you're tarnishing."

Anastasia didn't say anything to the outburst. She let it ride as she was talking about their mother and that would be something hard for anyone to take.

"Mom was wonderful, but mom had serious faults. One fault being when she thought that Cinda was vying for a position in the house. Cinda was happy to have us there. Mom's jealousy blinded her from that fact. We allowed it to blind us as well."

"How do you know that Cinda was happy to have us there? She never showed it," Drusilla argued with her.

"No, we didn't allow her to show it. We blocked her at every turn. Even after mom died, we kept mom's legacy alive. We were wrong. Admit it."

Drusilla opened her mouth to say something then shut it quickly again.

"You've come here after storming out of the hotel room and disturbed my birthday celebration. I asked you not to come here. Why can't you just be happy? You act as if you have a fucking stick up your ass."

"Looks to me as if you're the one who's had something in her ass. You're not only here with one man, I'm told, but with two. What the hell are you, a nymphomaniac?"

Anastasia fell into a peal of laughter, and Drusilla's expression was laughable.

"What the hell are you laughing at? Stop laughing at me," Drusilla said.

"I'm not laughing at you. I'm laughing at your choice of word. If I'm a nympho, I will take that role on gladly. I've never been happier with Lucien and Bruno. I plan to keep being happy, and if it means I'm a nympho, then get used to it."

"Ana, please. Just come back with me. We don't need anyone else."

"That's where you're wrong. We do need others. You act like a repressed prude."

"I'm not a prude."

"Prove that to me. Stay here and find someone to have a fantasy with."

"I ... I ... can't Ana."

"Can't or won't, Dru? There are plenty of men here at the club who are solo and wouldn't mind a beautiful woman on their arms. There are even women here who'd take a go at you." The light that lit Dru's eyes when she said women gave her pause. Bingo. Her sister wasn't as uptight as she'd always thought she was. Her sister liked women. There was nothing at all wrong with that.

"I can't," Dru said again.

"I'm sure that Flora wouldn't mind sharing a fantasy or two with you."

"Fuck no! Keep her away from me."

Ana watched Drusilla squirm in her chair. She'd let it drop for a bit.

"Dru, reconsider what I said about Cinda. That is the one thing I want you to do. No more of this anger over something that should never have been our fight. Please, I beg of you as my sister."

Drusilla's shoulders sagged. "Okay, okay. I'll think about it."

Anastasia got up quickly and wrapped her arms around Drusilla and hugged her tight.

"Oh thank you, thank you!"

"I said I'd think about it, Ana," Dru warned.

"I know, but I have faith you will turn around."

"I may be a lost cause."

"No way, Dru. We lost our way. I found where my path led, and now it's your turn to do the same. I say starting with Flora may be the perfect place to be led."

"What? Why do you keep throwing that woman at me?"

"Dru, you and I both know that you're physically able to have had her tied up. You're in martial arts. Don't tell me that she at about 5'5" overtook you and your 5'10"." Anastasia watched as Dru's cheeks turned pink.

"I didn't want to hurt her."

"There's no way you would have hurt her. You and I both know it. How I never realized that you were into women is beyond me."

Drusilla growled. "I don't like that woman."

"You could have fooled me. Like I said, you have to prove it to me."

"Ana, I have nothing to prove."

"So you say. Well, at any rate, it's my birthday, and my guys and I were about to have cake before you decided to crash the place. Want to come and have some and meet Lucien and Bruno?"

"Sure, why not." Drusilla shrugged. "Is Cinda here?"

"She may be, but I've been a bit busy."

Drusilla gave an unladylike snort and for the first time a smile spread across her face.

"I'm sorry for everything I've said to you." Drusilla spoke softly.

"I'm sorry too. We have a lot to work out, but one day at a time works for me."

"Yes, one day at a time. Sounds like a wonderful plan."

Anastasia undid the binding tape from Drusilla's legs first and then her hands. Drusilla massaged her wrists. This could have turned out a lot worse, so she would believe that everything would work out in the end. She would make sure that she put in for Dru's fantasy if Drusilla didn't.

"Come and have some cheesecake with me. We have a lot to celebrate, new beginnings for one thing and new desires that have been awakened."

"Ana, please ... stop, nothing has been awakened."

"Keep on saying that like you believe it. Come, the cheesecake I'm told is divine. I hope you don't mind the semi-dressed people and very nude people."

"If you can take it, I can take it."

"Well then, let's go." She held her hand out to Drusilla and once she took it she led her out of the suite towards her men. When they arrived back at the table, she had to hold back the laughter that was bubbling up. At the table sat Luc, Bruno, and Flora. She had to tug her sister forward and into the chair next to Flora.

The men stood. Lucien spoke up first.

"Everything okay?"

"Everything is fine, Luc. Drusilla has decided to celebrate my birthday with us and have some cheesecake. Glad you could join us, Flora."

The blonde smiled back. "Lucien and Bruno were kind enough to give me a drink after my little skirmish." Flora's gaze was directed at Drusilla who shifted in her seat yet said nothing. Then her cheesecake was brought to the table along with a large bottle of champagne, and she stopped focusing on what that gaze meant. Besides, that was for Drusilla to deal with. She clapped her hands in excitement as everyone at the table sang happy birthday.

****

Later that evening, tangled in the sheets in between her lovers, she sighed contentedly, her head on Lucien's chest and Bruno's head on her shoulder. This was how everything should be. She was happy, and now was the time to let them know how much.

"Lucien and Bruno, I love you. You've brought so much to my life, thank you."

Bruno kissed her shoulder, and Lucien kissed her on the mouth.

"I love you and Bruno as well, my sweet. I know I hurt you before. For that I'm sorry."

"No, don't be. It had to happen. I needed to grow up. I wouldn't have been ready for this, for us then."

"You're so generous with your forgiveness and your love, Red."

"I just know that there isn't time for regrets anymore. I don't want to regret anything. What happened with Cinda is proof enough of how things can fester."

"I love you both as well," Bruno said. "Lucien came into my life when I thought I wasn't ever going to find someone to love. Through his eyes I fell for you, Ana. Our family is complete."

"Until, that is, we decide to have children. Then we will be truly complete." Anastasia said. "I want children with the both of you. Two is a nice round number. I want one child from you, Lucien, and one child from you, Bruno."

"Red, you couldn't have made us any happier or made us feel any luckier than you have in this moment. Thank you."

"Yes, my sweet Ana, thank you."

They all hugged each other tight. Several kisses later, Anastasia discerned that their lives would never be the same, and that's how she loved it. She couldn't wait to see Doc Fairee to thank him for her second chance. Love would keep them together, trust would make sure they stayed that way, and the kink would bind them tightly.

The End

www.authornikkiprince.com

Evernight Publishing

www.evernightpublishing.com